In Your Dreams

The boy who could see the future

-by-

Bill Chandler

**All proceeds from the sale of this
e-book are being donated to
Crosby Area Foodbank**

http://crosbyarea.foodbank.org.uk/

For Sean and Ciaran,
my special boys

Author's note

I'm still wondering what on earth possessed me, a forty year old lawyer and father of two, to think that I could write a novel! Yes, I used to write short picture books for my boys when they were small, but those books have long since been outgrown. As a family we regularly enter the poetry section of the Sefton Writing Competition (and with a fair degree of success between us, if you don't mind me saying), but writing a whole book is a different kettle of fish entirely. But, having long promised the boys (and myself) a 'proper' book, I suddenly found myself with an unexpected surplus of time whilst I recovered from minor knee surgery. This book is the result of that time. Whilst the writing process at least saved me from the worst of the frustration that inevitably comes with temporary immobility, I'm still deciding whether it was time wisely spent from a literary perspective. Hopefully it will at least raise a few pounds for the important work of the Crosby Area Foodbank. Any feedback will be most gratefully received (and can be left on the book's dedicated Facebook page www.facebook.com/inyourdreamsbook), just in case I ever decide to embark on another similarly foolish endeavour. Thank you for choosing to read my book, I hope you enjoy it!

Bill Chandler
Crosby, August 2013

Chapter One

Ok, I know what you're thinking, it must be incredible to be able to see the future unfold before your very eyes before it happens. Mustn't it? I mean, it's only natural, so why wouldn't you think that?

Just imagine for a moment, if you can, being able to avoid any potentially difficult or dangerous situations and protect those people you love from harm. What gift could possibly be more precious or amazing than that?

I'm sure I would have agreed with you, once. But believe me, the reality of the situation is very different and my supposed gift also became my biggest curse. Which is why I'm asking you now, right at the start of my story, to keep an open mind on the matter until you see for yourself the chaos and devastation for which it was responsible.

If you'll excuse a slight diversion, that request reminds me of my good friend Jasper. Ever since I've known him, which is a very long time, Jasper has always had this habit of occasionally narrowing his eyes, lapsing into a fake Chinese accent and coming out with what I call 'the wisdoms of Jasper'. As you can probably guess, sometimes that can be mildly amusing, sometimes it's downright annoying but occasionally, just occasionally, Jasper can be pretty profound.

Anyway, one of the wiser wisdoms of Jasper goes something like this, "Jasper say, the mind is like a parachute, it works best when it is open". Jasper crops up plenty of times during my story, so you can make up your own mind about him!

There's one more thing we also need to be clear about from the start if we're going to get along. I'm sure the more cynical among you are already contemplating how you could use, or abuse, such a gift to make your fortune. As you will see, however, my own particular gift never revealed any lottery numbers, football scores or anything else from which a financial profit could be made.

Right, now that we've got all that straight, let's get on with my story

Chapter Two

I'm sure that, like me, you're keen to skip forward to the exciting parts where I get to see the future, but it is important that I put the story into some sort of context. Without understanding my early life, what follows would make no sense. So I implore you, please, to humour me and immerse yourself in my childhood.

The early years of my life were quite unremarkable.

I don't remember being born (who does?), but apparently I was born in Liverpool one wild and stormy night, and Liverpool certainly has plenty of those! I wasn't born in the nice new Liverpool Women's Hospital with the blue roof that's there now, which apparently churns out eight thousand babies a year in Europe's largest maternity unit. No, I was born in the old Maternity Hospital on Oxford Street.

I was an average baby, weighing just over seven pounds, the first child born to an average young couple. And yet, by all accounts, despite the averageness of my arrival (if there is such a word as 'averageness') my mother and father were extremely excited to see me and I was a much-loved baby.

After spending the first few days of my life in the hospital, my parents took me home to Crosby and in due course I was baptised in the parish church of St Cuthbert's by the energetic young priest Father Shivijan.

Don't worry if you haven't heard of Crosby, not many people have outside of the north west of England, although if you mention Crosby to people of my parents' age they will go all dewy-eyed and reminisce about Shirley Williams' legendary win for the fledgling Social Democratic Party in the 1981 by-election.

If you arrive in Crosby by train, you would be forgiven for wondering where they had put it. You see, the station is situated in a residential area a good half a mile from the actual village. I remember as a child asking my Dad why they hadn't built the station nearer the village.

"That's a very good question, Jimbob," he replied, "and apparently when they built the railway they did consider building the station near the village, but in the end they decided it was best to build it near the railway!"

Ok, so Crosby is hardly the centre of the universe, but it does have a lot going for it. Sitting at the northernmost extremity of the Liverpool suburbs, when I was a young boy Crosby had a beautiful sandy beach from which I could (and frequently did) spend hours watching the ships sailing in and out of the Mersey Estuary to my left. Or you could look straight ahead, across the top end of the Wirral peninsula, and admire the hills and mountains of North Wales. On a clear day you could even see the Great Orme at Llandudno and the snowy peaks of Snowdonia, the highest mountains in Wales. Or you could look to the right and just stare out at the vastness of the Irish Sea which extended infinitely towards the horizon.

Nowadays you can still see all those things, but the view from Crosby Prom (as the locals call the seafront pathway) has become so much busier.

For a start, the beach is now home to one hundred men. That's right, one hundred men! But you don't need to worry about their welfare. You see, they're not illegal immigrants, or poor souls forced out of their homes as a result of the 'bedroom tax'. In fact, I'll let you into a secret, they're not real men at all! They are the one hundred iron men who make up the 'Another Place' installation by Antony Gormley, the sculptor most famous for the Angel of the North in Gateshead. Stretching for nearly two miles along the beach, you either love them or hate them, and I love them. Depending on the tide and the light, they never look the same twice.

The other big change to the view is the windmills. The Burbo Bank Offshore Wind Farm opened for business in 2007 and now dominates the view from Crosby beach, whilst another windfarm can be seen in the distance on a clear day. Like the iron men, not everyone loves the windmills, but personally I think they add to the view, and at the end of the day you can't really complain about something that reduces our carbon emissions by over six million tonnes.

Crosby has also produced or been home to some really famous people. And, whilst I may not have been overly impressed that some grumpy female quiz show presenter went to my school or that I came from the same town as an Archbishop of Canterbury, I did have my Crosby heroes.

Roger McGough may have been born in Litherland, but he did go to school in Crosby, which is enough for me to claim him for Crosby. Roger (or, to be more accurate, his prolific body of poetry) always seems to have been part of my life. As a child, I adored poems like 'The Leader' when we studied them at school, and as I grew older I retained my love of his work and enjoyed the darker side of poems like 'The Sound Collector'.

I can't believe that there are many people who haven't read Roger's poems, but if you're one of them then I demand that you stop reading this book right now, pop down to your local library and seek out a collection of Roger McGough poems. Then, and only then, will I allow you to come back and pick this book up again! If you are reading this book in fifty years time and are wondering what a library is (or, rather, what a library was), they were fantastic public buildings where people could borrow real books to take home and read, before returning them for someone else to read. And it was all free.

But my absolute favourite Crosby hero must be Hank Bovril-Joyce. Regularly voted the coolest person in Crosby by our fantastic weekly local newspaper the Crosby Bugle, Hank wrote screenplays for Hollywood films and also wrote brilliant books like 'Hundreds and Thousands'. However, his finest moment came in 2012, when the World Tiddlywink Championships came to Britain for the first time in a generation. Hank excelled himself by writing the Opening Ceremony, which was universally acclaimed as the best opening ceremony of any event ever since time began, or at least since Emperor Titus joined The Rolling Stones on stage at the opening of the Coliseum in Rome in 80AD.

So, I hope that I've established that Crosby wasn't a bad place to grow up. At first there were three of us, Mum, Dad and me. We lived in a nice suburban three-bedroomed semi-detached house, about 10 minutes walk from the beach. Life was just perfect.

Then, a couple of years later, we were joined by a crying, screaming bundle of joy, my baby brother Jack.

Chapter Three

My Dad, real name Dale McLoughlin, was unremarkable to everyone outside our house. A man of average height and build, my childhood memories recall his mop of dark brown hair, which has long since faded to grey and now to white. A quiet man perhaps, but Dad was an optimistic soul, always confident that life would keep getting better and that "everything would turn out for the best".

Dad was a man of simple pleasures. I remember vividly the great excitement in our household every Thursday when the paperboy would post the latest odition of the Crosby Bugle through our letterbox. Dad took great interest in local affairs and would read out to the family any interesting stories which caught his eye.

There was also the great Nefty Sweeney mystery, with which Dad entertained us every week. What do you mean, you've never heard of the great Nefty Sweeney mystery? Well, if you're not from Crosby then I suppose there's no reason why you should. But if you are from Crosby, then no doubt you have read the Bugle at some point in your life. And if you have read the Bugle at any time in the past ten or twenty years, then you may have noticed that all the leading news stories are written by a journalist called Nefty Sweeney, whose name was the cause of much debate at our house.

"Nefty Sweeney," my Dad would say every week, "what sort of a name is that? I've travelled to the four corners of this planet and never heard of anyone called Nefty."
"But Dale, dear," my Mum would interrupt, "you've never been outside of Merseyside!"
"That may be so, but it's still a weird name. You can't even tell if it's a man or a woman!"
"Well I think it's a woman," said Mum, giving Dad a mischievous wink, "all the best people are!"
"And I think it's a man!" announced Dad, just wanting to be contrary.

That little scenario was repeated most weeks, and we would scour each edition for any evidence or clues which might help resolve the mystery.

Dad worked in an office in the great metropolis of Liverpool. To be honest, I was never entirely sure what he did. Every morning, he would head off on the train wearing the standard businessman's uniform of smart suit and tie and he would reappear each evening, usually just late enough to avoid having to play any part in the preparation of the evening meal.

If my Dad was the dreamer, my Mum was the realist, with both feet planted firmly on the ground. Mum's real name is Amy McLoughlin and she had given up work to look after me. To be honest, I don't think she meant to, it just kind of happened. One day you're working quite happily, the next day you have a baby and then somewhere down the line you just forget to go back to work. In later years, Mum threw herself into voluntary work, but it was nice having her around while I was growing up.

Mum was a few inches shorter than Dad, with a long mane of red hair and a freckled face which betrayed her Irish roots. She needed glasses to read, which she hated, and she was forever forgetting where she had left them around the house. I always thought of Mum as being pretty rather than beautiful, but it was obvious that Dad adored her and thought her to be the most beautiful woman who had ever lived.

And then there was little old me, James Robert McLoughlin of 33 Blundell Drive, Crosby. Known to most people as Jimmy, and to my Dad as Jimbob, I was a typical boy. Although I had inherited my Mum's red hair and freckles, I quickly grew into a strong and powerful little boy.

As a boy, I had four passions - sport, books, Lego and the family pets.

I was never happier than when I was playing sport, any sport. Dad taught Jack and me how to play football and cricket, in the back garden at first and then in the park as we grew bigger. Mum took us to swimming lessons, initially for our own safety so that we would be able to save ourselves if we ever fell into a river or a particularly deep puddle, but in time we both became very strong swimmers.

When I wasn't playing sport, you could usually find me with my head buried in a book. There were no Kindles in those days, we read real books made out of paper. I was a voracious reader and was forever tormenting Mum to take me to the library. The old Carnegie Library was only a few minutes walk from our house and was a fantastic old building, complete with a bell that we could hear chiming the hour from our house, so that even now I always refer to it as 'the chiming library'. I read recently in the Bugle that it has been declared an asset of community value, which is only right and proper.

Mum and Dad encouraged my reading and must have spent days of their lives, if not weeks, reading stories to me and Jack. I particularly enjoyed it when Dad read some of the old classics to me, such as the stories of the great detective Sherlock Holmes. I wanted to be like Holmes, solving impossible mysteries using nothing more than a magnifying glass and the power of deduction. I also enjoyed the science fiction books of authors such as HG Wells and Jules Verne, and I must have read my Dad's old edition of 'The Invisible Man' more than a dozen times.

When it was too wet to play out and I had read all my library books, I would turn to Lego for amusement. In those days, Lego was just Lego, not 'Star Wars Lego', 'Harry Potter Lego', 'The Only Way is

Essex Lego' or whatever the latest fad may be. In my day, Lego was simply a box of different sizes and colours of small coloured blocks that you could fit together to make things. The only instructions we had were those we invented ourselves, and what we could build was limited only by our imaginations.

We must have had thousands of Lego bricks, which lived in a huge wooden box in the meter cupboard under the stairs. Over the years, I must have made thousands of Lego models. I made cars, aeroplanes, space rockets, and lots and lots of buildings. I don't know why, but I always loved making buildings. Often I would build my own versions of iconic buildings like Tower Bridge, Big Ben or, closer to home, the Royal Liver Building in Liverpool. Other times I would build my own designs. Dad often joked that he wouldn't be surprised if I grew up to be a builder or an architect.

However, my Lego models never lasted long in a house which was also home to a younger brother crawling around and our two pets, Corky Dog and Rabbit.

Corky Dog was a black Labrador with patches of brown, the soppiest and loveliest dog I have ever met. Don't ask me why he was called Corky Dog, we all know there was a reason (and I'm sure it was a good one) but it seems to have got lost in the mists of time.

Corky loved his walks along Crosby Prom, especially if he got let off the lead for a run on the beach, where we used to play this game.

We knew that he wanted to run into the sea and he knew that we didn't want him to. So, he would pretend to run along the edge of the water, edging closer and closer to the point where he could just run in and have a good splash. One of us would keep calling him away from the water and he would make a token effort to come towards us before edging back towards the sea. We all knew that eventually he would get wet (and Mum would complain for days about how difficult it is to get rid of 'wet dog smell'), but it became part of our family tradition.

Rabbit, you will not be surprised to learn, was a rabbit. And a fat rabbit as well, quite the largest rabbit I ever saw. We obviously couldn't have been feeling particularly creative the day we named her. Rabbit lived in a wooden hutch in the back garden, and whenever Corky Dog was outside he would often go over to the hutch and just stare at Rabbit. Jack always used to insist that Corky Dog and Rabbit were married and, who knows, maybe he was right!

My little brother Jack was two years younger than me. Although physically similar to me, Jack was blonde as a baby and for some time as a child, but in time Jack's hair gradually darkened until it resembled Dad's hair. Which was actually quite ironic, because just as Jack's hair was darkening, Dad's hair was starting to get lighter!

Mum and Dad had made the time-honoured mistake of thinking that a little brother or sister would be good company for me and that we would be playmates. They had however merely created a rivalry that would lead to a lifelong power struggle. It is probably fair to say that Jack and I enjoyed the typical love-hate relationship enjoyed by so many siblings, especially brothers - we just loved to hate each other.

It didn't take long for the rivalry to reveal itself. Long before the tantrums over who had broken the other child's Lego model or who had kicked or thrown a ball at the other, I set the scene on my very first meeting with Jack. When Jack was born, you see, it took him a little time to grow into his slightly oversized ears and nose. Apparently, when I first saw him, I pointed at him and shouted "elfant". For many years afterwards I still called him Elephant, especially if I really wanted to annoy him!

I think my relationship with Jack disappointed both my parents, who wanted nothing more than for us to be friends. Despite all the arguing and fighting, Dad maintained in his usual optimistic way that Jack and I would realise as we grew up that we did have a special bond and would always be there for each other.

I must confess that as a child I never shared Dad's confidence. It wasn't that I didn't want to be Jack's friend but, as anyone with a sibling will confirm, it isn't always that easy.

Chapter Four

As you can see, my childhood was pretty uneventful. Apart from an exotic uncle, to whom I will introduce you shortly, I was a typical suburban child growing up in a typical suburban family. Life was happy (for the most part) and I had no inkling of how un-typical and un-suburban I really was.

So, when did I realise I had this special power and could see the future? It's difficult to say, for two reasons. Firstly, I'm sure all of us struggle to recall precise events and dates from our childhood memories. I'm sure we've all heard people say "well it must have been such and such a year, because I remember it was the year of the royal wedding or the silver jubilee or the great flood".

Secondly, you have to remember that even when I realised that I could see the future, I didn't appreciate how unusual that was. For a long time I assumed it was just a natural part of life, that knowing what was going to happen tomorrow was no more out of the ordinary than remembering what happened last week. It took me a lot longer to realise that not everyone could do the same.

If I think carefully, the signs were certainly there from an early age. One of my very earliest memories is of the four of us on holiday in a caravan in Cornwall. Jack was a toddler, which makes me probably no more than four years old, maybe five at most. Anyway, before we went on this particular holiday to Cornwall I can remember having a particularly vivid dream.

Jack had a lovely soft teddy bear, called Barnaby, who went everywhere with Jack. They were inseparable and if Barnaby ever got lost then Jack would be inconsolable. In my dream I could see very clear images of Barnaby lying somewhere which was grassy but also dark and low. I remember that making no sense to me, since I couldn't work out how anywhere could be grassy but also dark and low. I knew that grassy areas got dark at night, but I could sense that it wasn't that sort of dark, it was the sort of darkness that came from being in an enclosed space with a low ceiling.

I remember arriving at the caravan park just outside St Ives, and being so excited at the prospect of living in a caravan and the wide sweeping sandy beach below us. But more than anything I remember arriving at the caravan, walking up the steps to the door and noticing the area underneath the caravan. It was a grassy area, because the caravans had been positioned on the grassy ridge behind the beach and the sand dunes, but because it was underneath the caravan it was dark and scary, with a low clearance between the grassy floor and the bottom of the caravan. A space small enough for a boy of four years old, maybe five, to climb under, but not much more. Now it made sense!

One day during that holiday, Jack was crying and wailing uncontrollably. Mum picked him up and asked in her most concerned voice, "What's wrong, my little Jacky-Wacky?" but Jack could only sob into her dress. Eventually we were able to ascertain that Jack was distraught because he couldn't find Barnaby, which led to a thorough but ultimately fruitless search of the caravan and Dad's car.

Everyone was just about resigned to the fact the Barnaby was lost for ever when I remembered my dream of Barnaby in the spooky, dark grassy area. I opened the caravan door, walked down the steps and had a good look under the caravan until, sure enough, I saw Barnaby lying on the ground. He must have fallen out of Jack's hand, or maybe out of his pushchair, when we were going into the caravan. I quickly scampered under the caravan and out again, then back up the steps and into the caravan.

"Barnaby!" squealed Jack, running up to me and giving Barnaby a huge squeeze. There was no "Thank you Jimmy" or hug for me, mind you. It would have been nice to be appreciated but, to be honest, I didn't expect any thanks or reward. Jack was young and was simply delighted to be reunited with his best friend.

But if Jack was less than grateful, my parents' reaction was not pretty.

"How did you know Barnaby was under there?" asked my Mum, accusingly.

"Yes, you went straight to him," continued my Dad, before I'd even had time to respond to Mum, "like you knew exactly where he was!"

"But I did know exactly where he was!" I confirmed, not realising that I was making matters worse.

"So, you admit it!" shrieked Mum, "You hid Barnaby, just to upset Jack. I don't know why you boys can't just be friends."

"But I didn't hide Barnaby!" I protested.

But it was too late. In Mum and Dad's eyes I could only have known where Barnaby was if I'd hidden him, and there was no point trying to convince them otherwise. Great! I hadn't expected to be treated like a hero, but it seemed more than a little harsh to be treated like a criminal for saving my little brother's favourite toy. Parents can be so unfair!

Maybe that was why I didn't talk too much about seeing the future while I was growing up.

Chapter Five

Of all my relatives, the person I felt closest to outside of our house was Uncle Mo, or Uncle Mobo as I called him when I was very young.

Family legend decreed that Dad's sister, Auntie Minnie, had met Mohammed al-Ali whilst she was on holiday in Egypt and he was working as a tour guide escorting tourists around the magnificent remains of Ancient Egypt. They fell in love instantly, so the story goes, got married and settled in the suburbs of Manchester, about an hour away from our Crosby home.

So why did I find Uncle Mo so exciting? Maybe it was because he looked so distinctive. Uncle Mo certainly looked very different to the rest of us McLoughlins. Compared to the rest of us with our very pale complexions, Uncle Mo was positively dark. Not dark like all those Scouse girls who have spent too long under a sunbed, but the most fantastic and exotic olive colour that marked him out as being from the Middle East.

He was also the largest man I had ever met. Not quite a giant, Uncle Mo was certainly tall, but it was more than height alone that made him stand out. A strong, powerfully-built man, I never doubted the truth of the stories with which he would entertain me for hours about how he had wrestled man-eating lions in his youth.

Uncle Mo was also the only man in our family to have a beard. And what a beard it was, a big bushy beard that had been as black and as vast as deep space when I was a very small boy, but which had gradually become greyer (but no less vast) as I grew up.

And he had the most expressive brown eyes I have ever seen. One minute those eyes could be piercing, sometimes verging on angry, but they also possessed a rare ability to twinkle and smile. I always thought it was just as well that Uncle Mo's eyes were so expressive, because his mouth was so lost in his beard.

Or maybe it was the way Uncle Mo spoke that appealed to me. As you might expect, the rest of us sounded like we came from Liverpool, but Uncle Mo had the most entrancing accent. Everything he said sounded mystical and magical, even if he was only asking you to help him with the washing-up after a family dinner!

Uncle Mo also told the most exciting stories of far-off places and, what's more, he promised to take me to see them one day! I remember being on a train once with Uncle Mo, I can't remember where we were going or why, but we went through Stockport.

Anyone who has been through Stockport on the train will remember that you approach the station along the top of a massive Victorian brick viaduct with fantastic views either side, and as you cross high above the M60 Manchester orbital motorway, you pass an unusual blue pyramid-shaped building, which I think is now used by the Co-op Bank.

"Look, Uncle Mo!" I screamed with excitement, "a pyramid, a pyramid!"
"Yes, my boy", replied Uncle Mo, "so it is, and what a magnificent pyramid!"
"Is it like the pyramids in Egypt, Uncle Mo?"
"It has the same basic shape, but it is much more modern and much smaller. Back home in Egypt we have real pyramids, built amid great mystery thousands of years ago to house the tombs of the great Pharaohs of Egypt. One day, my boy, when you are older I will take you to see the Great Pyramid at Giza."
"Thank you Uncle Mo, I would like that very much."

Uncle Mo always called me "my boy", and it made me feel special. Uncle Mo and Auntie Minnie never had any children, so I think Uncle Mo treated me like the son he never had.

And whenever he spoke about Egypt, he always called it 'home' and spoke with great pride and passion. I wondered how someone could give up a place that obviously meant so much to him and where everything was so 'real', whether it was good or bad.

"That's not a beach, my boy," Uncle Mo once laughed when we visited Blackpool, "back home in Egypt we have real beaches that stretch as far as the eye can see, with warm seas that you can swim in all year round and fish of every colour you can possibly imagine, and some that you can't!"

Even when I complained about the English weather, I remember Uncle Mo retorting, "That's not rain, my boy, back home in Egypt we have real rain that hurts your head and nobody can leave their homes for days on end!"

I guess Uncle Mo must really have loved Auntie Minnie.

Over the years, Uncle Mo promised to show me lots more exotic places when I grew older, not just the pyramids but also the Sphinx, the Valley of the Kings, the Arabian Sea and lots more far-flung places. He even promised to take me to Mecca, the birthplace of the great prophet Mohammed after whom Uncle Mo was named. I couldn't wait. I frequently imagined us visiting all these incredible places together, although as much as I wanted to I would never dream about them. In the meantime, Uncle Mo took me to places closer to home but no less exciting, and I got my taste of the Middle East in the restaurants of Rusholme.

Chapter Six

Looking back, it seems like my special power was acclimatising me gently, starting with minor things like a lost teddy bear and gradually over the years working up to more serious incidents. That's probably another reason why I didn't think too much of it as a child.

The first time I can remember foreseeing anyone getting hurt was my best friend Jasper.

I mentioned Jasper earlier, but I think it's time I introduced you to him properly. Jasper was my best friend. I can't remember exactly when we first met, because our mothers took us to so many of the same baby activities, like Tumble Tots, Kinder Music, Baby Bungee and Toddler Skydive. Ok, I might have made those last two up, but had they existed then I'm sure that my mum and Jasper's mum would have taken us! It was therefore quite unsurprising that Jasper and I recognised each other on that fateful first day at St Cuthbert's Primary School and quite quickly struck up a strong friendship.

When you're four going on five, you never realise how the friends you make then will affect the rest of your life. A week is a long time for a four year old boy and you can't imagine being at senior school, let alone a grown up. But for so many people, the friends they make at primary school remain friends into their adult life, and so it was with me and Jasper.

In truth, we actually shared little in common, not least in appearance. Jasper is what we now call mixed-race, his father having been brought up in Liverpool's Afro-Caribbean community in Toxteth before moving to Crosby when he married Jasper's mother. Jasper's dark skin and jet black hair contrasted vividly with my red hair, pale complexion and freckles. I was tall, but I don't think Jasper ever grew taller than my shoulders. I was strong and powerful, but Jasper just looked like he'd eaten too many pies.

It was the same at school. I wasn't the brightest child in our class by any stretch of the imagination, but I was certainly above average, whereas Jasper always struggled academically. That always confused me, because to me Jasper was the cleverest and funniest person I had ever met. He may not have been able to list all the prime numbers up to one hundred or spell tricky words, but his imagination was always brimming with creative ideas. Jasper would entertain me for hours with all the characters he had invented, each having its own personality and accent.

Although we both enjoyed being active, our interests rarely converged. Despite claiming to have Jamaican ancestry, I think Jasper would have struggled to walk one hundred meters in those days, let alone run it! So, whilst I was outside kicking a football around, Jasper would be inside practising his martial arts. Jasper tried virtually every martial art I had ever heard of, from karate to taekwondo and from kung fu to aikido, but his real love was judo, at which he excelled.

The martial arts also gave Jasper's imagination the chance to run riot, giving rise to his most enduring character, the oriental sensei. Whenever I asked Jasper the secret of his success at judo, he would narrow his eyes and say, in his best mock-Chinese accent, "Jasper say, to control the body, one must first learn to control the mind!"

Despite our differences, or maybe because of them, we remained firm friends. But our friendship was by no means exclusive. As well as the separate friends we each acquired through our sporting activities, we were also fortunate to have some other fantastic boys in our class. At breaktime you could usually find us running around with Alfie and Paddy, playing some new game that Jasper had invented and we would all be happy to go along with.

Alfie was the cleverest of us all. He never got into trouble and always kept his uniform immaculate, even after the roughest football matches on the playground. But despite being a gifted child he also managed to remain 'cool', and he was kind hearted enough to help the rest of us out if we were struggling with difficult spellings or the intricacies of long division.

Paddy, by contrast, was the class clown. Although he was even smaller than Jasper, Paddy more than made up for his diminutive stature with a huge personality. Paddy was cheeky and funny in equal measure but never in a way that could cause any real offence.

Those early years at school seemed to last forever. Not in a bad way, you understand, just in that way that time seems to speed up the older you become. But eventually we reached that age, around ten or eleven, where we were starting to be allowed the freedom to go places and do things without our parents being around. It was our last year at primary school and our parents realised that once we started senior school they couldn't insist on taking us everywhere all the time.

We enjoyed our newly found freedom to the full. It was a different age back then and our parents were happy for us to play out, so long as we were back home before dinner was on the table. During the school holidays we had the whole day to explore and we usually made the most of it. I would cycle to Jasper's house and then we'd meet up with Alfie and Paddy. Sometimes we would go to the beach, sometimes to the park, or if the weather was nice we would see how far up the coast we could cycle before getting tired.

And so it was in the October half term holiday. We were conscious that the winter would soon be upon us and the four of us were determined to have one last big trip out before the cold weather and dark evenings restricted our mobility. We thought that if we set off early enough and carried a picnic lunch in our rucksacks that we should be able to make it all the way up to the seaside town of Southport, a dozen miles or so to the north. We probably wouldn't have the time or the energy to cycle back, but the train from Southport to Crosby has always been cycle friendly and in those days it didn't cost much to bring four boys and their bikes back home.

A couple of nights before the big adventure, I had another vivid dream. Jasper was crying, but in a way that I had never seen anybody cry before. I could tell that he was in pain rather than upset, but I couldn't tell where, when or how he had got hurt. I woke up in a cold sweat but assumed it was just a nightmare. I didn't make the connection with the vivid dream I had experienced in Cornwall, maybe because of the time that had elapsed or maybe because the content of the two dreams was so different.

The following night, having packed my Dangermouse rucksack with drinks, snacks and the all important crisp and tomato ketchup sandwiches, I was too excited to sleep. I tossed and turned, went to the toilet, crept downstairs for a glass of water, tossed and turned some more and went to the toilet again before eventually dropping off to sleep.

As I began to dream, I saw Jasper again. Once again he was crying, but this time I could see more. He was lying in the grass, next to his bike, holding his left knee. He had obviously fallen off his bike and his knee appeared to be bleeding quite badly. Once again I woke up in a cold sweat, but it still didn't occur to me that the dreams were premonitions of what was awaiting us on our big adventure.

At 8 o'clock the next morning we met, as arranged, outside the old swimming baths by Crosby Prom. I was the first to arrive, followed shortly after by Jasper and then Paddy and Alfie arrived together. It was a beautiful day and the early morning sun glistened on the sea water as it lapped upon the beach. There was no sound except for a few seagulls who screeched overhead; it felt like we were the only people alive and the whole world belonged to us.

"Right then," began Jasper, "have you all brought some grub with you?"
The rest of us nodded.
"And your mums all know we're out for the whole day?"
The rest of us nodded.
"And we're all agreed that we're trying to make it to Southport before it gets dark?"
The rest of us nodded.
"You're all very quiet," remarked Jasper, "has anyone got any questions?"
"Yes," piped up Paddy, "are you sure you know the way to Southport?"
Jasper narrowed his eyes and retorted in his best mock-Chinese accent, "Jasper say, only a fool can get lost on a straight road!"

And so it was that four friends and their bicycles left Crosby on a grand adventure. We made good progress northwards along the coast to Hightown and soon we were cycling through Formby's magnificent pinewoods. We were relying on Jasper's sense of direction and didn't question him when we left the main path and took a more cross country route through the woods.

Maybe we should have questioned Jasper's wisdom, because that was when disaster struck. As we cycled through an area littered with pine cones and other debris, Jasper's bike hit a fallen tree trunk and came to an abrupt stop. Jasper however did not stop. He kept hurtling forward for another twenty yards, flying through the air over the handlebars and over the fallen tree before crashing back to earth.

"Jasper!" we all screamed in unison, "are you all right?"

There was no answer. More frightened than any of us had ever been before, we all rushed over to where Jasper was lying. Thankfully, Jasper was alive but he was crying in a way that I had never seen anybody cry before, except in a dream. And he was holding his left knee, which was bleeding quite badly.

"What do we do?" shouted Paddy.
"Firstly, we keep calm," said Alfie, "we're no good to him if we panic. Jasper, do you think you can move?"
"Noooo!" cried Jasper.
"In that case," continued Alfie, "Jimmy, you need to stay with Jasper. Me and Paddy will go and find help."

I'm sure they weren't gone long, but to me it felt like an eternity. Fortunately, Jasper's pain seemed to subside by the time that Alfie and Paddy returned with an elderly couple they had found who had been out walking in the woods. The grown-ups bandaged up Jasper's injured knee with his handkerchief and helped us get safely to Freshfield station and on a train back to Crosby.

As we all sat in silence on the train, I reflected on the events of that strange morning. Obviously I was relieved that Jasper's injuries weren't more serious, but I had also made the connection with my dreams of the previous two nights. I now realised that I was capable of seeing future events before they happened, although I still didn't appreciate how unusual that was.

Chapter Seven

I don't seem to have mentioned Mum, Dad and Jack for a while. Yes, I cherished my special times with Uncle Mo and my adventures with my friends, but most of the time it was just the four of us.

You might be surprised to hear me say that was just fine with me, but I enjoyed our family time. Yes I was good at arguing with any - or sometimes all - of them, but at the end of the day they were my family and I loved them all. Even Jack. One of my favourite things was hearing my dad call out, "Jimbob, Jack, do you fancy a run out to the park?" or my mum inviting us out for a walk to the beach.

We couldn't always all stay friends for the entire duration of the trip (and sometimes we could even manage to fall out before we left the house because Jack and I were so slow at putting our trainers on), but many of my happiest childhood memories involve those simple local family excursions.

It was during that period that I developed my reputation as a weather forecaster. As I've said, my gift was still developing while I was a child and it started giving me a unique insight into the weather. Not everyday of course, that would just have been freaky, but just whenever we were planning something special.

This is how it worked. Whenever we had a free weekend coming up, Mum and Dad would usually ask me and Jack to think whether we had any suggestions for trips out. I would then dream that night what sort of day it was going to be and I would make suggestions accordingly. So, I would suggest that we should go to Blackpool on bright sunny days, fly kites on windy days and visit museums on grey and wet days.

I never mentioned how I chose my suggestions, because I simply assumed that was how everyone else worked. Which was why I was so surprised that Jack insisted on going to Southport on his ninth birthday to walk along the pier and play crazy golf. I wasn't disputing his choice of activities, since the delights of Southport were something we could always agree on, but I couldn't comprehend why he would want to go there on such a wet and stormy day. In my head, you see, I knew exactly what the day would be like and I assumed that Jack did too.

Chapter Eight

The next time the dreams took a more sinister turn involved Uncle Mo. I mentioned earlier that Uncle Mo and I shared a special bond. He wanted someone to whom he could tell all his wonderful stories of exciting adventures in exotic far-off lands and I was more than happy to listen. I really did believe that one day we would travel together to North Africa and the Middle East and he would show me all the magical places he had told me about.

In fact, I felt sure that I could find my way around the region myself, since Uncle Mo's stories painted the scenes so vividly in my young mind that even now I sometimes find it difficult to believe that I haven't actually been there.

But not long after I started senior school, there were quite different scenes etching themselves into my mind. At first I struggled to understand and interpret the vivid dreams I was experiencing. I dreamt that Uncle Mo wasn't well, which made no sense to me because whenever I saw Uncle Mo he was still the same strong man I had always known.

And when I started dreaming of Uncle Mo without his beard, I was really confused. Confused at first because I simply didn't recognise him without his beard. I had never realised before how much Uncle Mo's beard defined not only his appearance but his whole character. Without his beard he looked weak, like a modern day Samson shorn of his locks, and strangely naked. Confused also because the one thing I knew about Uncle Mo was that he would never get rid of his beard. Never. Not ever.

Despite my previous experiences with Barnaby and Jasper, I still didn't realise that these ominous dreams were premonitions. With the benefit of hindsight I can't believe how foolish I was, but I attributed the strange dreams to the changes which were occurring in my life at that time. The transition from being the kings of primary school to bottom of the heap at senior school was not an easy one. The jump from year 6 to year 7 may not sound like a major leap, but anyone who has been through it will understand what we were all going through that autumn.

Sefton High School was a nice enough school. In fact, it was more than nice. A fantastic Victorian building, it enjoyed wide sweeping staircases, never-ending corridors and ridiculously high ceilings. It was however much further from Blundell Drive than St Cuthbert's had been.

"Jasper, it's miles away!" I complained one day.
"No, it isn't," retorted Jasper, "and anyway, don't be such a wimp. You're supposed to be the energetic, sporty one, remember?"

"Yes it is," I continued, "I don't even think it's walking distance, we may have to get the bus!"

Jasper narrowed his eyes and adopted his mock-Chinese accent.

"Jasper say, anywhere is within walking distance, if you have the time!"
"JASPER!!!!"

A definite plus was that we were all together. Miraculously, I had been placed in a class with my best friends Jasper, Alfie and Paddy. It was just like the old days. Except that as well as the children from St Cuthbert's, Sefton High was also full of children from Crosby Primary, St George's and several other local schools. I had never seen so many children as that first full school assembly. And they were all bigger than us!

There was also the small matter of having different teachers for different subjects and having lessons in different classrooms. Some of the teachers were quite strict and shouted a lot, but there were some nice ones too. My favourite was the PE teacher, not just because I loved sport but because he was so cheerful and positive. Yes he could sometimes be a little prickly, who can't, but it was easy to see why he was known by the kids simply as Mr Sunshine.

And of course there was the joy of homework. We used to think we got lots of homework at St Cuthbert's, but in hindsight we didn't know we were born. The days of coming in from school and relaxing soon became a distant memory as we quickly realised that senior school was serious business.

Jasper in particular seemed to be overdoing things on the homework front. I didn't see much of him outside of school that first term, since all his spare time was being spent producing copious amounts of very impressive homework.

"Jasper," I challenged him one lunchtime, "what's with all this homework malarkey? You're making the rest of us look bad!"
"Well, it's all right for you," Jasper replied, "you're bright, but you know I'm not very good at school. I need to make a good first impression so the teachers think I'm a good worker."
"But you can't keep up this sort of pace forever, you'll burn out. Doesn't Jasper usually say, why do today what can be put off until tomorrow?"
"Usually, but this is different," Jasper continued, narrowing his eyes. "Jasper say, the man who gains a reputation for getting up at dawn can lie in bed until midday!"

You see, Jasper really was so much brighter than everyone gave him credit for, even me. He had realised that a strong start that first term would establish a reputation that would hopefully keep the teachers off his back for much longer.

With all that happening, it was perhaps unsurprising if my brain was taking the opportunity each night to cut loose and go a little mad. And that was why I was dreaming of Uncle Mo without his beard. Wasn't it?

However, as my friends and I gradually got to grips with finding our way from Maths in room 14 to History in room L3, my dreams didn't improve in the same way. In fact, the dreams became darker and scarier. By Christmas Uncle Mo no longer featured in my dreams, with or without his beard. The dreams now focussed on Auntie Minnie, whose cries haunted me each time I awoke.

It was over the Christmas holidays that Mum and Dad sat me and Jack down for a 'chat'. Normally that meant we were in trouble, but this time their mood was different, sombre and subdued rather than angry.

"Boys", started Dad, "I'm afraid we have something to tell you."
I could tell it wasn't good news.
"It's about Uncle Mo", continued Mum, "I'm afraid he's not very well. It will be difficult for you to understand, but he's not going to get better. So you need to be gentle with him and accept that he won't be able to do all the things he used to."

This was bad news. Seriously bad news. I could tell that Mum was struggling not to cry as she told us. I couldn't believe it. I didn't mind if we couldn't go to Egypt or Mecca (or even Stockport), but Uncle Mo had to be there for us. And if I felt that devastated, I couldn't imagine how poor Auntie Minnie must be feeling.

The next time we saw Uncle Mo he looked fine, but over the next few months he became weaker and weaker. The treatment he was undergoing at the hospital resulted in him losing all his hair, and I knew that losing that magnificent beard was the hardest thing of all for him to take. Although he stopped looking like himself, his eyes still twinkled and smiled and he kept his humour right up until the end.

I last saw Uncle Mo quite near the end, and it was an emotional encounter.

"I shall miss you, my boy," began Uncle Mo.
"Not as much as I'll miss you", I replied.
"I'm just sorry that I'm letting you down," he continued.
"You could never let me down, Uncle Mo!"
"But I promised to take you to see Mecca and now I won't be able to. I hate breaking promises. Maybe one day you will make it there yourself and, if you do, maybe you will spare a thought for me and say a prayer."
"Yes, of course, Uncle Mo. I will go there one day, I promise."
"The only promise I want from you, my boy, is that after I'm gone you will be kind to Minnie for me."
"But I don't want you to go, Uncle Mo!"

I had been struggling to hold it together and at the point a flood of tears erupted from my eyes and started flowing down my face. I gave Uncle Mo a big hug and kissed him on the cheek. It struck me that it was the first – and only – time that I ever kissed Uncle Mo. As a boy I had kissed all my other relatives, except for my great friend Uncle Mo. I think perhaps his beard had always discouraged me, I simply wouldn't have known where to aim!

"Now, I don't want you being upset," he said calmly, and I admired how he could be so calm when my little heart was breaking. "I have been the luckiest man alive to do all the things I have done, to see all the things I have seen, to meet all the people I have met – including you, my boy – and to have found true love. Many people spend their whole life searching for peace and happiness, but I have found true contentment. Please try, for my sake and Auntie Minnie's, to concentrate on the fantastic times we have spent together rather than dwell on the times we will not have. I have enjoyed our times together and I have no doubt that you will achieve great things, my boy."

Uncle Mo was the first person I had been close to who had died, and I was distraught for a long time after. A lot of people were, since it was only after his death that I realised how well known and how well loved a man he was. I felt helpless and more than a little guilty; after all, I had seen it coming but hadn't understood the warning. But I consoled myself with the knowledge that, even if I had realised what the dreams had meant, there was absolutely nothing I could have done to prevent it.

So I took comfort in the thought of Uncle Mo looking down on me from above, guiding and protecting me. Uncle Mo's twinkly eyes were now stars twinkling in the night sky. I told my best friend

Jasper how I was feeling and for once the wisdom of Jasper seemed quite profound:

"Jasper say, it is only in darkness that we can see the stars."

Chapter Nine

It was a beautiful late autumn day when Mum uttered the immortal words that would change my life forever.

The sky was bright blue, the air was crisp and it was one of those rare days where you could see Mount Snowdon, in all its snow-covered glory, from the beach at Crosby. A red-amber glow was beginning to emerge from the horizon, signalling the onset of one of those fabulous autumn sunsets with which the west coast of England is blessed, and an observant onlooker would have noticed a not-quite full moon already visible in the late afternoon sky.

Whilst I would have loved to be that observant onlooker, sadly I was oblivious to such wonders of nature. Instead, I was sat at the dining room table in Blundell Drive trying to finish a particularly challenging Maths homework assignment. I had struggled with Maths ever since joining Sefton High and I always found the homework incredibly difficult.

I was sitting there among my books, with the contents of my pencil case randomly scattered across the table, when Mum strode into the dining room on her way through to the kitchen. I was engrossed in my studies and my gloomy mood deteriorated even further when Mum started tidying up my mess.

"Leave me alone, Mum," I protested, "this is hard enough without you fussing around me."

"Sorry love," apologised Mum, "but I could see you ending up getting that sharp compass stuck in your hand and I just wanted to put it away before you got hurt."

Suddenly, my mood lifted. Mum had moved the compass to stop me from getting hurt. Now, if you're wondering how anyone could get hurt by a tool for finding magnetic north, you're thinking of the wrong sort of compass. Think again of the viciously sharp implement designed to assist the drawing of perfect circles, but which had become the weapon of choice for generations of schoolboys. And my Mum had moved mine to protect me from pain and injury.

"Thanks Mum," I blurted out, and Mum seemed more than a little surprised at the degree of my appreciation.

By this time, several months after Uncle Mo's death, I had finally accepted that I could sometimes see the future in my dreams, but I didn't think I could influence events. I was also still labouring under the misapprehension that everyone had the same ability as me. So, it didn't strike me as odd, or as a simple figure of speech, when Mum said that she could see me getting hurt from the compass, I thought she had really foreseen it. But what amazed me was that, having foreseen my injury, she then prevented it by removing the danger! Clever Mum!

My head flooded with a hundred questions. How could I have been so impossibly stupid? Why had I assumed that I could not influence events? Indeed, what was the point of being able to see the future – and so far it had largely been bad parts of the future - if you couldn't do anything to change it?

I may not have been on the road to Damascus, but in that one sentence - "I could see you ending up getting that sharp compass stuck in your hand and I just wanted to put it away before you got hurt" - Mum had suddenly, albeit inadvertently, changed my whole outlook on life. Just think what I could achieve if I now viewed my premonitions as warnings, helping me to save those I loved from harm!

Saving those I loved from harm? A darkness fell over me as I remembered Uncle Mo and the visions I had dreamt long before he became ill. Was I to blame for Uncle Mo's death? Could I have saved him if I had acted upon those dreams? I wished with all my heart that I had known then what I knew now, but Uncle Mo was gone and I couldn't go back and make things better. All I could do was to make sure that I never allowed anything similar to happen again.

Chapter Ten

Armed with the knowledge that I could change the future, for the first time ever I was eagerly awaiting the next dream. Fortunately, I did not have too long to wait.

Jasper had been visiting our house after school. We had finished our homework and Mum had cooked us a delicious spaghetti bolognese with garlic bread. There was still a little time before Jasper had to go home, so we had ventured out into the garden.

"What shall we do?" I asked, "Would you like to play football?"
"Jasper say," commenced Jasper, in his mock-Chinese accent, "Life without football is like a blunt pencil …. pointless!"

Even though Jasper was not really the sporty type, he was always happy enough to kick a ball around in the garden. I groaned at his comment and kicked the ball at him, hitting him right in the tummy. Jack heard us playing and came out to join us, followed shortly after by Corky Dog. Rabbit watched us from her hutch, twitching her nose occasionally. Now that we were growing up and had discovered computer games and football, Rabbit received much less attention than she used to, but that didn't mean that we loved her any less.

Soon it became dark and Jasper's Mum arrived to walk Jasper home. We said our goodbyes and then Jack and I went inside. After the obligatory bath and toothbrushing session, it was time for bed. I read for a short while and then turned out the light and lay my head on the pillow.

And so it all began. I fell quickly into a deep sleep and began to dream. I dreamt of Rabbit, which was not surprising since I had just been playing out in the garden. But in my dream Rabbit was not sitting happily in her hutch, twitching her nose occasionally and wondering where the next carrot was coming from. No, in my dream she was lying on her side, her snow white fur tarnished with what looked like blood. She wasn't moving and if she was still breathing then it was imperceptible.

The focus of the dream then moved to another creature. A larger creature, but definitely not Corky. This was an evil wolf-like creature, although my mind was unable to process exactly what type of animal it was. But, whatever it was, it was sniggering, almost laughing, at the atrocity it had committed.

I awoke in a cold sweat. In my agitated state I strove to recall every detail of the chilling dream. Poor Rabbit, what evil fate was in store for you? I pulled the curtains back and in the moonlight I was able to satisfy myself that no harm had befallen Rabbit. Yet.

The next morning at breakfast I raised the subject with my Dad.

"Dad, I'm worried that Rabbit's going to be attacked by a wolf or something."

"Don't be silly," Dad replied, "there are no wolves in Crosby. And anyway, Rabbit's been out there for years and she's never come to any harm. That's a strong hutch, I made it myself."

Suitably reassured, I set off for school, but I still couldn't help worrying all day. I explained my fear to Jasper, and outlined my plan to save Rabbit, but if I'd been hoping for a sensible discussion then I was sadly mistaken.

"So, I'm going to check Rabbit from my bedroom window every night before I go to sleep and get up very early every morning to make sure Rabbit is all right."

"How early?"

"I don't know, I haven't figured that part out yet, but early enough to check on Rabbit before breakfast."

"I don't like getting up in the mornings."

"Neither do I, normally, but this is an emergency situation. And, as they say, the early bird gets the worm!"

"Worm? I thought we were talking about Rabbit?"

"We are! It's just a saying, like the wisdoms of Jasper."

The moment I said it, I knew that it was probably a mistake to mention the wisdoms of Jasper when I was trying to formulate an important plan. Sure enough, Jasper placed his hands together and adopted his mock-Chinese accent.

"Jasper say the early bird may get the worm, but it's the second mouse who gets the cheese!"
"JASPER!"

And that's how I ended up conducting a vigil on Rabbit's hutch. Of course, I had no idea when – or even if – the attack was going to happen.

Some basic research had confirmed that Dad was quite correct that there were no longer any wolves in Britain, although there did seem to be some doubt as to precisely when and where the last British wolf was killed. A carved grey stone next to what is now the A9 trunk road near Brora in Scotland commemorates the death of the 'last' British wolf in 1700, although apparently it seems likely that wolves continued to roam for a good half a century after that. But, all the same, it seemed unlikely that wolves had survived undetected for over two hundred and fifty years, only to blow their cover by savaging an ageing pet rabbit on the Sefton coast.

Nonetheless, the dream was quickly becoming a regular programme and the laughing wolf haunted my sleep. I could only presume that as the dream became more vivid, the event was coming closer.

Then, one dark and dirty night, it happened. I had my bath, as usual. I dressed in my pyjamas, as usual. I brushed my teeth, as usual. I went to my bedroom, as usual. I picked up my binoculars, as usual. I pulled back the edge of the curtains and looked out, as had become usual.

But the sight that met my gaze was certainly not usual. A large, grey, wolf-like creature was attacking Rabbit's hutch, its paws tearing at the mesh. Dad's sturdy hutch was putting up a good fight, but it was clearly no match for the ferocious attacker. I had to intervene if Rabbit was to be saved.

"Rabbit!" I screamed, at the top of my voice. I ran downstairs and flung open the back door. Then I froze. The creature did not flee as I expected, but turned round and looked at me. It looked old and raggedy, with a nose that had obviously seen better days. It seemed to taunt me, challenging me to do something, and all the while the evil laugh from my dreams was ringing in my ears.

Dad arrived at the back door, to see what the fuss was all about. He instinctively put his arm out and pulled me behind him, out of the direct line of sight of Rabbit's nemesis.

"Be careful Jimbob, stay here," Dad commanded, "he's a big one, and he doesn't look like he's scared of us."
"See Dad, I told you a wolf was coming for Rabbit."
"That's not a wolf," explained Dad, "it's just a fox, but he's so old and dirty that he looks a bit like a wolf, especially on such a grey night."
"Save Rabbit," I implored, "please, Dad."
"Of course," Dad reassured me, "we just need a plan."

But before Dad could think of a plan, we were both blown out of the doorway by a tornado emerging from the kitchen. The tornado burst out into the garden, barking like never before, and headed straight for the fox. I feared what would happen next, but the tornado managed something that Dad and I had failed to achieve. A look of fear awoke in the eyes of the fox and he turned and bolted for his life.

"Corky Dog saves the day, hurray!" shouted my little brother, who had also been attracted by the kafuffle.
"Good boy, Corky," I called out, "you're my hero!"

I ran out into the garden and gave Corky a big hug. He was excited, running round and round and yelping with joy. He knew exactly how much his actions had meant to all of us.

Then I rushed over to the hutch. The fox had made a mess of the mesh, but had not fashioned enough of a hole to threaten Rabbit, who had taken refuge at the back of the hutch. I picked her up and talked to her in my most reassuring voice as I carried her into the house.

"Don't worry Rabbit, it's all going to be all right. Corky Dog has saved you from the nasty fox!"

I was delighted. We had saved Rabbit's life. But more than that, for the first time in my life I had acted on my dreams and changed the story. Tonight proved what I could achieve if I could understand my dreams and develop a plan to eliminate the danger.

"We'll find a box and some blankets inside for Rabbit tonight, "said Mum, "she's had quite a shock." Even though Mum had never been Rabbit's biggest fan, she had a big heart.

"And I'll fix the hutch first thing tomorrow," said Dad. "I'll make it even stronger this time, although I don't think we'll see that fox round here again after the chasing off Corky gave it!"
"Which just proves what I've always maintained," chuckled Mum, "that Corky has a thing for Rabbit!"
"Yes," interrupted Jack, "they're married!"
"Well, I don't know about that," said Dad, "but I would like to know how you knew that was going to happen, Jimbob?"

Chapter Eleven

That was the night that I finally realised how special I really was. As you know, I had always assumed that everyone else could see the future too. I hadn't even the slightest inkling that I possessed a unique gift.

So, when my Dad enquired how I knew that Rabbit was going to be attacked by an animal resembling a wolf, I told him. I mean, why wouldn't I?

"I saw it in a dream, Dad."
"You what?"
"I said I saw it in a dream. In fact, I had the same dream several times, each time more lifelike than the last."
"And you expect me to believe that?" roared Dad.

I think it was at that point that the penny began to drop that Dad didn't have dreams like that. Maybe that would have been the perfect time to change the subject, but foolishly I continued digging.

"Yes, Dad," I replied, "have you never had a dream of something that was going to happen, and then it happened?"

"Well actually no, I haven't."

"Mum?"

"No Jimmy, me neither."

"Jack?" I asked, more in hope than expectation that my little brother would come to my rescue.

"You're a freak! Jimmy's a freak!" Jack never failed to disappoint me.

"But Mum, what about when you moved my compass the other week because you could see me hurting myself on it?"

"Oh no dear, I hadn't had any sort of vision, I just saw it lying in a dangerous place and didn't want to take the risk of anyone getting hurt. The same way that I might move toys if you've left them on the stairs, or a cup of hot tea perched too close to the edge of the table."

I was incredulous. Nobody else could see the future? How could I be the only one? Why me? I wasn't sure that I wanted to be special. So, once it became apparent that Mum and Dad didn't share my dreams, I thought it best to start playing it down. They may not have believed that I was telling the truth, but they were happy to classify it as a one-in-a-million coincidence.

That night, I lay in bed wondering what to do next. If I told Mum and Dad about all the other things I had dreamed, including Uncle Mo, they couldn't possibly denounce it all as just a coincidence, could they? They would have to believe that I really could see the future, wouldn't they? Or maybe they would refuse to believe me and get cross?

I didn't feel ready to take the chance. After all, I'd saved Rabbit, proved that the future could be changed and discovered that nobody else seemed to share my gift. That was more than enough for one night!

Chapter Twelve

For a long time after the incident with Rabbit and the fox, I kept my secret to myself. Mum and Dad didn't mention it again and I think that over time they even forgot that I had ever suggested something as fantastically ludicrous as being able to see the future. I knew that they couldn't cope with that particular truth and – let's face it - if my own parents couldn't accept it, then how could I possibly expect anybody else to believe me?

My problem, of course, was that my gift didn't go away. For me, it wasn't simply a case of trying to ignore what had happened and move forwards. For me, the crazy reality was that I had a peculiar gift which was constantly reminding me of its presence, but which I couldn't mention to anyone. I was living a secret double life and, as anyone who has ever kept a really big secret will tell you, over time the secret begins to eat away at you. When Dad gave me the book 'The strange case of Doctor Jekyll and Mister Hyde' as a present, it almost became too much for me to bear.

And if it wasn't enough that I was hiding this massive secret from my family and friends, the dreams themselves began to trouble me. I still had normal dreams like everyone else, of course, so I was constantly trying to distinguish between what was a normal dream and what was a premonition. That was usually easy enough, since the premonitions had a distinctly different feel to them. They inevitably began with a sense of foreboding, a general dark and sinister feeling. However, despite being particularly vivid they were usually more abstract than normal dreams, so I had to devote a lot of mental energy to interpreting them.

When my special dreams were at their most regular, I would become frightened to go to sleep. I would lie awake at night, tossing and turning and doing whatever I could to force myself to stay awake. At that time, I would have given anything to make the dreams go away forever. I felt like the most cursed person who had ever walked this earth, like an outcast. And because I couldn't tell anyone what was happening inside my head and how bad it was making me feel, I felt so alone.

I grew more and more distraught and exhausted with every month that passed, and as my strength diminished I was spending more and more time ill. My school work began to suffer, to the extent that eventually the headmaster had to call my parents into school to find out why my results had nose-dived. My permanent tiredness made me so grumpy that my friends started spending less time with me, including my best friend Jasper. Even Mr Sunshine became frustrated with me, and the final straw came when my lack of energy resulted in the usually chirpy PE teacher assigning me a new position on the school football team … left inside.

I was at my wits end, scared about what was happening to me. I knew I couldn't carry on like this forever, but I really didn't know where to turn. One night, as I lay on my bed sobbing myself to another frantic sleep, I knew that I needed a friend. A friend who wouldn't judge me or mock me, someone with whom I could be completely honest and who would in return give me some rational advice.

Since I didn't know anyone who satisfied that description, I invited Jasper back to our house after school the following day. I didn't choose Jasper just because he was my best friend, although that was obviously a factor. I also chose him because, when I had finally allowed myself to drift off to sleep the previous night, I had experienced a dream where I had told Jasper my secret and he had believed me. I was sure it had been one of my special dreams, but I was still extremely nervous as we walked back from Sefton High School to Blundell Drive.

When we got there, we discovered that Mum had cooked us some tea. Jasper ate the meat and potatoes, but refused any other vegetables.

"Jasper say, no peas for the wicked", was his inevitable response. I'm not sure that my Mum knew quite what to make of Jasper.

Talking about making things, after tea we built the Taj Mahal (the famous Indian monument, not the restaurant in Waterloo) out of

Lego. Then I sat Jasper down and told him everything. And I mean everything, from first to last. I asked him not to interrupt me while I spoke, and to be fair to Jasper he respected that request. He sat there, staring at me more and more intently, his brown eyes growing larger and larger with every revelation. When I had finished speaking, Jasper still sat there silent and motionless, just staring at me. Maybe I had hypnotised him?

"Jasper," I prompted him, "it's ok for you to talk now. What do you make of it all?"

Jasper narrowed his eyes, joined the fingertips of each hand together and gave me his wisdom in his very best mock-Chinese accent.

"Jasper say, no man can know the future!"

So, my family had refused to believe me and now my best friend too. I realised now why I had kept my secret to myself for so long. Suddenly, I felt more scared and more alone than ever.

But Jasper had kept his fingertips together and his eyes narrowed. His wisdom was not yet fully imparted and he continued in his mock-Chinese accent.

"But you is not man, you is boy. And Jasper say, if boy wants his dreams to come true, at some point he must wake up."

I wasn't sure whether I entirely understood what Jasper meant by that last comment, although if truth be told I'm convinced that even Jasper doesn't always realise the true meaning of his wisdoms. In any event, I wasn't sure whether I wanted *all* my special dreams to come true, but I interpreted Jasper's wisdom to mean that I could no longer continue burying my head in the sand and hoping that this madness would all suddenly go away. Instead, I would have to face up to my demons and find a way to deal with them.

Looking back, that day was a massive turning point in how I handled my condition. Talking it all through with Jasper had been a therapeutic experience in itself, but going forward it made the world of difference just knowing that somebody else understood what I was going through and that I didn't have to keep everything to myself for the rest of my life.

Chapter Thirteen

Jasper's acceptance of my peculiar situation enabled me to start taking control of my life again. It was still difficult not being able to talk to my parents about it, of course it was, but I was suddenly able to maintain a more positive outlook on life.

I had lost a lot of time, more than I had thought, and I had a lot of catching up to do. My schoolwork in particular would need some drastic improvement to get back on track. I hoped that I might have a helpful dream where I got to see the exam papers in advance, but no such luck! The only dream that ever helped me at all was one where I dreamt that I'd left my calculator at home on the day of the big maths exam! Talking to my friends, it seemed I wasn't the only person to have that dream, but I certainly made sure that I had everything I needed each day before I set off for the next exam.

I scraped through my GCSEs, but did enough to be allowed to stay on and study for 'A' levels. Two more years at Sefton High beckoned for me and all my friends. We had all grown up so much since those days at St Cuthbert's, but one thing that hadn't changed was our friendship. Now that I was happier, any issues between us had been consigned to history.

By the time we started the sixth form, I had decided what I wanted to do with my life. My lifelong fascination with interesting buildings led me to want to become an architect. I hoped that one day I might be able to design something as iconic as the Royal Liver Building or the tower at Canary Wharf which had just been completed. I could remember my Dad telling me when I was very young that I should become an architect, and it looked like he had got it absolutely right. And I thought I was supposed to be the only one who could see the future! Too bad he still couldn't solve the Nefty Sweeney mystery!

Firmly back on track by now, I did well enough in my 'A' levels to take up a place on the Architecture course at York University. York is a beautiful city and I was extremely excited to be going, but I was also sad to say goodbye to my family and friends.

When the day came for me to catch the train to York, Mum really tried to be brave, but inevitably she ended up crying. I hated to see her upset, so I promised to call her as soon as I arrived.

Dad wished me well and gave me a big hug. He said it made him feel old having a son who was old enough to leave home and go off to university. It suddenly felt like a lifetime ago that I had been that little boy at Blundell Drive playing Lego with my Dad and listening to his bedtime stories. As pleased as I was to have grown up, there was also a part of me that missed those days. But I knew, even without a dream to tell me, that the bond I had established with Dad in those early years would last a lifetime.

Jack and I shook hands. We had remained friends, of a sort, but our childhood experiences and my inability to share my secret with him meant that we had never become as close as Mum and Dad had hoped when we were small. He promised to come and visit me, but he never did. And by the time that I returned three years later, Jack had gone off to Bristol to study modern languages.

That autumn also marked the breaking up of my friendship group. Jasper, Alfie, Paddy and I had been so close for so many years, but now we were spread to the four corners of the earth. Or, at least, to the four corners of Britain. At the same time that I was heading over the Pennines to York, Jasper was off to study Oriental Philosophy in Cardiff and Alfie was moving to London to work for a bank. Paddy had struggled academically but was strong and hard working and, with North Sea gas at its peak, he had found himself a job on an oil rig near Aberdeen.

I wondered when the four of us would next all be together again.

Chapter Fourteen

When I arrived at York, I threw myself into student life. I worked hard, determined to fulfil my dream of designing fantastic buildings. The irony was not lost on me that I was studying the art of designing beautiful buildings in the post-Apocalyptic dreariness of York's university campus. But how wonderful it was to be a student in that most historic of English cities, walking along the Roman walls and exploring the magnificent Minster on a free afternoon, or sitting among the field of daffodils beneath Clifford's Tower on a beautiful spring evening.

It was at York that I first began to take an interest in the environment. The green lobby was not as powerful then as it is now, but people were already starting to worry about the hole in the ozone layer. I was fascinated by what this might mean for all of us in the future and I was already beginning to wonder what I could do about it. When the press talked about global warming they inevitably focused on the evils of cars and aeroplanes, but it seemed to me that buildings would also have a role to play in saving the planet.

It was at a meeting of YES (the York Environmentalists Society) that I first met Jemima and Dan. Jemima was studying zoology and was becoming concerned at the effect global warming might have on animals. The changing climate is a real threat to many species and nowadays even comedy folk band the Lancashire Hotpots are singing about it, with their song 'Don't make the polar bears cry'.

Dan was American, and it showed. A big fan of gingham shirts and leather waistcoats, he kept his cowboy hat on so much you would have thought it was attached to him. If he had come into the room wearing spurs on his boots, I don't think anyone would have batted an eyelid.

Jemima, Dan and I became firm friends and we could regularly be found out and about campaigning about various environmental issues. One weekend we might be protesting against nuclear power, the next we might be lying in the mud in front of bulldozers trying to prevent inappropriate development which could spoil our beautiful countryside.

Jemima was only a small girl, quite tiny in fact, but I loved how she always seemed to be smiling. I was delighted when, after we graduated, she took a job at Chester Zoo. Chester Zoo is not only the best zoo in the country, and therefore a wonderful place for a young zoology graduate to be based, but it is also less than an hour from Crosby. Dan, unfortunately, had to return to Minnesota and we never saw him again.

After three years of working hard and playing hard, I was thrilled to graduate from York with my Architecture degree. I had come so close to going off the rails completely at Sefton High, but I had recovered and achieved something special. But, although I had thoroughly enjoyed my three years in York and had made many new friends, there was also a part of me that was glad to be going home once again.

Chapter Fifteen

Having been away for so long, I now saw my home town through fresh eyes. Everything seemed new and exciting, and it wasn't just that some things had changed, like the iron men who had arrived on the beach whilst I was away. No, even something as familiar and timeless as the smell of Satterthwaites bakery seemed more enticing than ever.

It was on one of my walks to pay my respects to the iron men that I bumped into an old friend.

"Jasper!" I exclaimed, "I didn't expect to see you here."
Jasper narrowed his eyes, as he had done so many times before, and spoke in a much-improved mock-Chinese accent.
"Jasper say, it is a small world, but you wouldn't want to Hoover it!"
I laughed. It was reassuring to know that three years away hadn't changed him in the slightest.
"I thought you were still in Wales," I continued, "When did you get back?"
"Only yesterday, I'm just seeing what's changed in my absence."
"Me too. Crosby's looking well, isn't it?"

"It sure is. Have you heard anything from Paddy or Alfie lately?"

"Yes. Paddy's still on the oil rig but is hoping to come home for a couple of weeks at Christmas. Alfie's up this weekend if you'd like to see him. He says the bank is a good place to work right now, big bonuses too."

So that's how we all came to be drinking hot chocolate in the Copper Kettle cafe in Crosby village that Saturday morning. We missed Paddy, but to make up the numbers Jemima caught the train up from Chester to join us. I was worried that Jemima might find it difficult to infiltrate our gang, bearing in mind how long we'd all known each other, but everyone tried hard to include her in the conversation and she fitted in perfectly. It was as if she'd known us all her life. From that moment on she was one of us and would regularly attend our little gatherings and join us on our excursions.

Elevenses turned into lunch and then after a stroll through Coronation Park we all made our own way home. Jasper and I were heading in the same direction, so we walked together.

"How are you doing Jimmy?" asked my oldest friend. "You look well and you sounded fine today, but do you still have, you know?"

"The dreams?"

"Yes, the dreams. Can you still see things before they happen?"

"Sometimes, but it doesn't scare me any more. Thanks for believing in me all those years ago."

"Jasper say, that's what friends are for."

"Did you learn that on your Oriental Philosophy course?!"

"Very funny. Have you told your family yet?"

"No, you're still the only person who knows."

"You need to tell them Jimmy, you really do. They need to know who you really are."

Jasper was right, of course. But, no matter how far I had come, I still wasn't ready to make that final leap of faith.

Chapter Sixteen

Having returned to Liverpool following my graduation, I accepted a job working for a fledgling studio in the city centre. My boss was an experienced architect called Arnie, who was (and I'm pretty sure he won't mind me saying this) a bit of a character.

Arnie had worked for many years at one of the large multinational practices, and what appealed to me was that he had worked on many of the most innovative schemes of the last twenty years, both in Liverpool and beyond. Now, Arnie wanted to be his own boss and had recently branched out on his own. But he had retained sufficient contacts, and an unmatched reputation for brilliance, that he was still being instructed on major projects.

I was also attracted by Arnie's lifelong commitment to sustainability and energy efficiency, which had manifested itself long before green issues had become trendy. We know now that our buildings are responsible for around half of our carbon emissions, more than plane travel and cars. Improving the energy efficiency of our buildings has therefore become a priority, but at university, Jemima, Dan and I had all been labelled as idealistic tree huggers (I preferred the term 'eco-warriors'). In Arnie, I had discovered a kindred spirit and together we would save the planet, one building at a time.

Working with Arnie was an education, in more ways than one. Rejecting the stereotyped image of architects as wearing tweed jackets and Hush Puppies, Arnie would arrive at the office most days wearing a football shirt. In summer he would wear the full kit, whilst his sole concession to winter weather was to add a matching football scarf to the ensemble.

There was a third member of the team, but I quickly gave Bob the nickname 'The Invisible Man' because he was never in the office. Arnie explained that Bob preferred to work as close as he could get to the site he was working on. Apparently Bob believed that he derived his energy and inspiration from talking to the site and breathing in the same air where his building was going to be 'born'.

Given my own individual circumstances, I suppose I wasn't really in any position to comment on someone else's peculiarities. However, in spite of myself, I couldn't help regarding this eccentric man of mystery with suspicion, although I couldn't help but admire his original designs, which were certainly innovative and extremely popular with clients.

At that time, Bob seemed to be spending most of his time in Formby. He was working on the new 'Pinewoods' housing estate which was being built on the site where the red squirrel reserve used to be, before they all caught squirrel pox and died. Whilst Arnie and Bob vehemently disapproved of the destruction of the magnificent woodlands, they accepted the commission on the basis that being involved in the project would at least allow them to minimise the environmental impact of the development. And so they retained as many trees as possible, used those that were felled as timber for the new houses and even managed to persuade the client to include a sanctuary for the rare Natterjack toads which inhabit the area. I couldn't believe that Formby Woods, which had been our playground as kids and where Jasper had so memorably injured his knee, would soon be lost forever.

As well as buildings, I loved to draw people. My notepads were covered in portraits of work colleagues, friends, family and sometimes even the occasional celebrity too. One day, to fill an idle moment in the office, I attempted to draw Bob. But there was one huge obstacle in my path, what does the invisible man look like? It was an unusual exercise for me, but strangely liberating, to put my creative spirit to work inventing a new person rather than a new building.

A short while later, I approached Arnie's desk clutching a sheet of A4 sized drawing paper.

"This is what I think Bob likes like," I announced as I showed him my sketch.

'My' Bob wasn't the most glamorous man you could ever meet and my drawing made him look interesting rather than handsome. I had given him a full head of unkempt curly brown hair and a full but similarly wild beard. His facial features were soft and kind and I had tried to capture the kind of twinkly eyes that are usually the exclusive preserve of favourite uncles. I had dressed him in a bold Paisley-patterned shirt and for some strange reason I had felt the need to complete the ensemble with some old dungarees. One hand held a paintbrush, while the other grasped a bottle held high in the air above his head. Whilst I had not intended this effect, the positioning of his arms and legs made it look as if he was dancing.

"Not bad," smiled Arnie, "considering you've never met the man! Although from what I know of Bob he would be unlikely to be dancing a jig like that."
"But that's just my impression of what Bob looks like," I said. "On the other side of the page is what he really looks like. Would you like to see it?"
"Yes, indeed I would," confirmed Arnie, sounding genuinely interested.

Slowly and deliberately, I turned the page over to reveal .... nothing! Absolutely nothing.

"I present Bob the Invisible Man," I proclaimed, pointing proudly at the blank page in front of us. I couldn't help laughing, and Arnie couldn't help joining me.

"Jimmy McLoughlin, I really should know better by now than to let you take me in with your silly jokes," he giggled, "but I have to admit that was good."

So I hope you can see why I was so happy to be working with Arnie.

Chapter Seventeen

Throughout this period, I felt it best to continue to keep my gift hidden from everyone except Jasper. Since our time in York, I had always imagined that I would eventually tell Jemima too at some point. But she was now close friends with Jack, who had finished his degree and was once again living in Crosby. Rightly or wrongly, I feared that if I divulged my secret to Jemima, that she would then tell Jack.

In truth, it wasn't too difficult to keep my dreams secret, since most of the dreams related to relatively innocuous events which I was able to influence without arousing undue suspicion.

Mostly I got things right, but sometimes I got them wrong.

Like the winter I dreamt of Dad slipping on the ice down by the station and breaking his wrist. I was determined to save Dad from this minor injury, but I had no wish to reignite the whole debate by explaining why.

So I kept an eye on the weather forecast, to identify the most likely day for the accident. Since Liverpool and its suburbs are coastal, we are largely protected from the excesses of the winter weather and experience far less snow and ice than other northern cities such as Manchester and Leeds. The local forecast indicated that there was one day, a Thursday, when the Sefton coast was likely to suffer extreme wintry conditions, and I drew up my plan accordingly.

On the Wednesday evening, I called Dad on the telephone.

"Hi Dad"
"Hello. Is that you, Jimbob?"
"Yes, Dad. Can I ask you a favour?"
"You can ask!" That had always been Dad's standard response to that question, but a response that I had never fully understood.
"It's just that there's a site in Bootle, off Hawthorne Road, that I need to inspect first thing in the morning. I was wondering whether you'd mind driving in instead of taking the train, and then you could drop me off on the way? And you'll probably be glad to be in the car since the weather's supposed to be grim tomorrow."
"No problem son, I'll pick you up at seven thirty."
"Thanks Dad, you're a star!"

Those unfamiliar with the area may still recognise the name Bootle, since for many years it was home to National Girobank. Football fans may also know it as the home town of the famous centre half Alvin Martin, who played nearly six hundred matches for West Ham over a period of twenty-one years and also played for England in the 1986 World Cup in Mexico. None of that was relevant to my plan, however, but Bootle sat nicely about halfway between Crosby and the city centre.

And so the following morning Dad duly collected me and dropped me off in Bootle before proceeding to his office in the city. And tonight he would drive safely home again. I was therefore feeling suitably smug, despite the icy wind which chilled my bones as I waited at the bus stop on Hawthorne Road for a number 52 bus to take me into the city. Of course there was no early morning site meeting, it had all been a ruse to keep Dad away from the train station on that treacherous morning.

You will therefore imagine my surprise when I rang Dad that evening to thank him for the lift. There was no answer at teatime, which was unusual. There was no answer at 7pm either. And by the time there was no answer at 10pm my concern was no doubt apparent from the worried message that I left on my parents' answerphone asking them to call me immediately on their return, whatever time. It was at times like this that I really wished my parents would join the twenty-first century and get mobile phones!

It was about midnight when Mum rang me. She sounded worried.

"Hello, Jimmy?"
"Hi Mum, is everything ok? I was getting worried."
"Sort of. We've spent the evening at Fazakerley Hospital A&E, your silly Dad has fractured his wrist falling over on the ice."

"What? Is he all right?"

"Yes, he's fine. They've put it in plaster and given him some strong painkillers. And I suppose there's worse things he could have done."

"But how did it happen, and where?"

"He did it down by the station. He'd stopped off on the way home to pick up this week's Crosby Bugle from the kiosk."

Of course, the Crosby Bugle comes out every Thursday and the kiosk at the station was the nearest place to buy it. I suppose I should have anticipated that, but I can't be expected to think of everything, surely?

I went to bed feeling relieved, frustrated and guilty in roughly equal measures. Relieved that Dad was going to be all right in the end. Frustrated that despite my best endeavours I hadn't managed to stop him breaking his wrist on the ice by the station. And guilty because if it wasn't for me he wouldn't have been at the station, with his car, at that particular time.

Various questions ran amok in my head, to which I would never know the answer. Was I responsible for Dad's accident? If I hadn't made him drive, would the accident have happened anyway? Or had I changed events to make it happen? And would the legendary Nefty Sweeney write a news story about the man who had broken his wrist in his desperation to buy the Crosby Bugle on an icy Thursday afternoon?

Chapter Eighteen

Looking back, maybe I should have realised that all the incidents which had occurred up to that point were building up to some major event. At the time, however, a series of relatively minor events seemed more than enough to deal with.

There was also the risk of complacency. Every time a few months passed without any vivid dreams, I would begin to fool myself that maybe there would never be another one.

And so it was after the incident with Dad and the ice. I didn't have another premonition that week. Or the week after. Or the week after that. Months passed, and the months became a year, and I remember thinking to myself, "This is the longest I've been without seeing things for as long as I can remember, maybe that's it?" But I was mistaken, big time. The dreams hadn't gone anywhere, they were merely building up to the big one!

It started as nothing more sinister than a bad dream, offering no detail of what might be happening, when, where or to whom. These bad dreams continued, but the sense of darkness and desperation steadily increased. By the spring, my sleeping hours were haunted by a general sense of foreboding and dread. Then, one night, the vision began to reveal itself to me.

I had arrived home late from work, excited about a major project I was working on with Arnie. For several months, the big news story across the country had been that buildings were beginning to crumble as the result of a deadly attack by a new form of acid rain. In the usual way, scientists were working hard to tackle the symptoms rather than the cause and they were now trialling protective coatings for buildings. But for many historic buildings, it was too little too late.

Media interest had unsurprisingly centred around London. Saint Paul's Cathedral was going to need a new dome, Tower Bridge was completely beyond repair and the Royal Family had decamped to Windsor Castle whilst the structural integrity of Buckingham Palace was tested.

Many other buildings around the country were similarly threatened, including in Liverpool the iconic Royal Liver Building. In many ways the ultimate symbol of Liverpool, instantly recognisable around the world, the Royal Liver Building had sat proudly at the Pier Head for a century, topped with the famous Liver Birds.

Now the building was crumbling. Patch repairs had been attempted, but the city was facing up to the reality that the deterioration could not be arrested and nothing could be done to save this grand old building. The occupiers had all been moved out for their own safety and the Liver Birds had been removed and were being stored in a safe but undisclosed secret location.

But, as they say, every cloud has a silver lining. If the Royal Liver Building was going to have to be demolished, it would need to be replaced. And any replacement taking its place among the famed 'Three Graces' UNESCO World Heritage Site would need to exude the same grandeur as the original, reflecting the personality of the city and providing a new home for the Liver Birds.

Arnie's reputation had brought the job to our door and we were at that exciting stage of developing concepts for the new building. At this stage we could be as creative, or as wacky, as we wanted. We were playing with shapes, colours and textures. It was certainly a challenge to design a modern building which would sit easily alongside the classical grandeur of the Cunard Building and the Port of Liverpool Building, the design for which was originally intended to be a cathedral. A challenge maybe, but also a once in a lifetime opportunity.

You will understand then why I was so excited that evening. After eating some hastily-prepared dinner and checking my emails and messages, I had spent some more time sketching out ideas before eventually heading up to bed. My head was literally buzzing with ideas.

I'm sure that I fell asleep as soon as my head hit the pillow and that's when it started. It began with the same sense of darkness and foreboding to which I had almost become accustomed, but this time it was different. I could see a person, although I was struggling to identify who it was because the face was fuzzy and blurred. I needed to know who was in danger, but in my sleep I was powerless. I awoke with a start and shouted out in my frustration, "Who is it, just let me see them!"

A cup of tea and a slice of toast later, I had calmed down, to an extent. I was caught up in so many emotions. I was disappointed that the dreams had come back, and with a vengeance. I was frustrated that I could not work out what I was being warned about. And I was scared, really frightened, because I could sense that this time it was more serious than ever before. This wasn't about a teddy bear being lost under a holiday caravan or some unpleasant but ultimately minor injury. This felt like it might even be a matter of life and death. Of course I had dreamt about death once before, but that was a very long time ago and before I had realised that I could influence events. This time it would be very different.

But what if I couldn't interpret the dream and someone met some awful fate because of my incompetence? Now I was getting myself over-excited again. I don't know why, but I felt the need to give myself a good talking to, out loud, even though I was the only person in the apartment.

"Calm down Jimmy McLoughlin, you're not going to help anyone in that state.

"Yes, you're quite right, it's annoying that you can't work out what's going to happen and no you can't stop it if you don't know what it is.

"But you have to trust the dreams. You get these dreams for a reason and they've never let you down yet, have they? You just have to relax and believe that the answer will reveal itself before whatever disaster happens."

It's not like me to speak so much sense, especially at night, but I knew I was right. I went back to bed, but I was restless and lay tossing and turning for what felt like hours. You must know what it's like when you really want to go to sleep, but the more you try the more you can't!

Eventually I did get back to sleep and in time the dream restarted. I had hoped that I had just paused the dream and could continue from where I had left off, but no. It was more like when you take a DVD out to clean it and then when you put it back in the machine you have to start again from the beginning. But in my situation I didn't even have the benefit of a fast forward button or a 'scene select' option on the menu.

After what felt like an eternity, the blurry face started to come into focus. There was still something wrong with the image, although I couldn't quite put my finger on what it was, but at least the identity of the figure was about to be revealed.

I remember experiencing a feeling of recognition, a sort of "Yes, of course it's you," but then the world was shattered by an incredible noise.

Chapter Nineteen

BBBBBRRRRIIIIIIIIINNNNNNGGGGGGGGG!!

The earth shattering noise was in fact my alarm clock, heralding the arrival of another day. Now I'm not a morning person at the best of times, but that morning I was angry. How could the alarm have gone off right at the moment that I was being shown who was in trouble.

I cursed my alarm clock and was about to launch it across the room (please don't make any jokes about time flying, this was a most serious situation), but even in my anger I could not bring myself to destroy the alarm clock I had owned since I was a boy.

I ate a restless breakfast, wracking my brain constantly throughout in a futile attempt to replay the dream in my head and work out who it was. I knew I knew them, but that didn't really help me. Every premonition I had ever experienced involved someone close to me.

Frustration quickly turned to fear. Twice that night I had missed an opportunity to discover who was in peril. Would fate give me a third chance? What if that was it, game over? Even if fate was generous, would it be too late? What if the awful event, whatever it was, was going to happen today?

I went to work as usual, but it's fair to say that my mind was not on the job. Arnie could sense the change in my mood and seemed genuinely concerned. Obviously I couldn't explain why I was so distracted, so I just told him I had slept badly and was tired. All of which was true enough, but Arnie knew me well enough to know that I wasn't being entirely straight with him.

It was with a sense of relief that the working day ended and I could go home. I spent the evening checking my mobile phone, the internet and the television news. I even watched the replays of the news with the little man in the corner doing sign language for deaf viewers. It was the smart man who usually entertained me with his incredible range of exaggerated facial expressions whilst signing, but tonight I took no pleasure in his performance. All that mattered was that nobody seemed to have come to any harm.

Having rung Mum and Dad, Jack, Jasper and Jemima to confirm that all was well, I went to bed. And sure enough the dream started again. This time however I did not wake up and in due course the blurred face was revealed to me again.

As the face grew larger and came into focus, I could see that it was Jack, my little brother. I remember thinking that there was still something wrong about the image, but I still could not identify what it was.

It was definitely Jack, but that was all I could make out. The sense of danger was stronger than ever, but there was no clue as to where he was or what was going to happen. He appeared against a dark, featureless background which told me nothing.

I slept surprisingly well in the circumstances, as if making up for the previous night, so when I eventually woke up I was sure that I hadn't missed anything. Yet, although I had seen the full dream this time, I still felt none the wiser. I knew I had no choice but to trust that I had been shown all I needed to know at this time and that more would be revealed to me before I needed to act. With that thought firmly implanted in my mind, I found it easier to go to work that day.

That night I rang Jack for a chat. Since returning from Bristol, he had struggled to make use of his degree and he was now working as a shop assistant in the Co-op by the College Road roundabout. He maintained that still gave him plenty of opportunity to use his language skills. He insisted that there were people living in Crosby who originally came from Peru, Paraguay and Outer Mongolia, not to mention a whole family from France who were living in a haunted house near the seafront for a year.

Although things had never been particularly great between us, we still kept in touch and met up from time to time. That particular night I needed to know that he was all right, so whilst speaking I casually asked him what his plans were over the coming week. I hoped that the answer to that question might reveal an obvious high risk activity on which I could concentrate my efforts.

"Nothing special," came the reply, "I'm skint until payday so I won't be going far. TV and xbox for me for the next week!"

I offered to buy him a pint in the Crow's Nest on the Saturday night. I wanted to keep him close for the time being, partly in the hope that I could protect him but also because I was scared at the thought of losing him. I recalled how heartbroken I was after Uncle Mo died and I couldn't bear the thought of losing my own brother. If I'm entirely honest, my feelings for Jack that night caught me somewhat by surprise.

Anyway, Saturday was only two day away, so that was all right. Nothing could happen between now and then, could it?

Chapter Twenty

I woke up on Saturday morning with a feeling bordering on excitement. Tonight I was seeing Jack and the absence of any more dreams must surely mean that there was nothing more I needed to know yet and therefore nothing to worry about today.

I wasn't even bothered that I had to go to work. Because of the need to progress the New Liver Building, Arnie had decreed that we couldn't afford to take the weekend off. I didn't feel that I could complain after losing focus during the week.

And so it was that I found myself in work on a Saturday morning. Arnie and I enjoyed a positive and productive 'creative meeting' and then went back to our desks to develop the ideas we had discussed. But the more the day went on, the more I felt distracted again. This was different, though, it wasn't the same distraction as earlier in the week when my mind was elsewhere, this time I was perfectly focussed on my work but just had this overwhelming feeling of tiredness.

By lunchtime the urge to sleep had become too much and I just had to rest my head on my desk. I instantly fell into a deep sleep, although the speed and intensity of the sleep actually made it feel more like a trance.

The vision of Jack returned, but this time with an even greater sense of immediate danger. For the first time I realised what was wrong with the image. Jack's features were blurred and his hair was floating up to the sky. Except it wasn't the sky. I noticed bubbles coming out of Jack's mouth and rising slowly upwards. Jack was underwater! That realisation explained everything. But where was he?

The dream released me and I jumped straight up. There was no time to stretch and rub my eyes. If the dream couldn't wait for tonight and had felt compelled to put me to sleep during the day, that could only mean one thing, that the danger was real ... and now. There were so many questions floating around in my brain, but I didn't have time for them now, I was on a one man mission to save my brother.

I grabbed my mobile phone from my jacket pocket and called Jack. I needed to warn him. Surely I just needed to tell him to keep away from water until I could get there! His phone rang several times before Jack's familiar voice cut in.

"Hello, you've reached Jack McLoughlin. I'm either busy or ignoring you, but leave your name and number after the beep and you never know, I might call you back!"

No, why couldn't he have just answered?

"Jack, it's me, Jimmy," I stuttered into the phone, "please call me if … when you get this message, it's important."

I tried the landline too, but no answer there either. I called Mum and Dad, but they hadn't heard from Jack and didn't know where he was. So, I had absolutely no idea where Jack was, but deep down I knew that I was the only person in the whole world who could save him.

My instinct was to head home to Crosby. Without putting my coffee mug in the dishwasher (Arnie was a stickler for doing things properly) or even closing down my computer, I literally ran out of my office and straight into Arnie.

"I've got to go, it's my brother Jack, he's in trouble" I spluttered.
Arnie was as cool, calm and collected as ever. "Of course, I hope everything's all right."
I was already half-way to the door when Arnie called after me.
"Let me know if there's anything I can do to help, and keep me posted!"
"Will do," I shouted back, with one foot already out of the front door.

I don't think I appreciated at the time just how good and patient a boss Arnie was. He liked to exude the mean and moody persona of another famous Arnie, and I was already tiring of him saying "I'll be back" every time he popped out for coffee or lunch. But, when push came to shove, Arnie was less like Arnold Schwarzenegger and more like a teddy bear!

I hailed a black cab on Dale Street and spent the journey trying to contact Jack. Where could he be? How could I save him if I didn't even know where to find him? As the cab hurtled over the Seaforth flyover, it struck me that I had absolutely no idea where I was going or what I should do next.

Chapter Twenty One

I directed the taxi driver to my parents' house in Blundell Drive and paid him fifteen pounds. As he turned the taxi and drove off, I rang the bell and banged on the front door until Mum answered the door.

"What's wrong, love?" asked Mum, "you look like you've seen a ghost!"

"It's Jack, he's in trouble, I've got to find him."

"What sort of trouble?"

"I don't exactly know," I admitted, "I think he's going to drown."

"Drown? How? Where?" asked Mum, visibly worried.

"I don't know, Mum, I don't know anything and I'm running out of time."

"I don't understand, love, what makes you think he's going to drown?"

"I saw it in a dream."

"Oh," said Mum, and I could sense her mood suddenly change from one of concern to one of frustration, "not you and your dreams again, I thought you'd grown out of all that."

"No Mum, this is real, don't ask me to explain but I know that something really bad is going to happen to Jack if I don't find him and find him quick."

"Quick-ly," piped up my Dad, who had been attracted by the commotion and was now standing behind Mum.

"Dad, this is no time for a grammar lesson!" I snapped as I turned and left the house.

It was obvious that Mum and Dad weren't going to be much use to me. It wasn't their fault, how could I expect anyone to believe that I could see things before they happened? I knew it sounded crazy and for a split-second I even wondered myself whether I was simply going mad.

Then I remembered poor Jack. This was no time for doubts, the dreams had never been wrong before and I couldn't ignore a dream as sinister as this one had been. Even though Jack and I were hardly best friends, at the end of the day he was still my brother and I couldn't let anything major happen to him. I could analyse things as much as I wanted once I knew Jack was safe, but for now I just had to keep on searching.

But where? I stood outside my parents' house not knowing where to go next. I checked my mobile phone again, but there were no messages. I needed inspiration.

I don't know why, but I suddenly remembered the Sherlock Holmes stories that Dad had read to me as a child. When I was young, I had wanted to be Sherlock Holmes, solving seemingly impossible mysteries. Now I was him, with a case of my own to solve. Sherlock Holmes wouldn't have floundered, he would have known exactly what to do and where to look. What was it that Holmes use to say? That if you ruled out the impossible then whatever you were left with, however unlikely, must be the truth.

So, I donned my imaginary deerstalker hat, smoked my imaginary pipe and considered what I knew:

1. I knew that Jack was broke and so couldn't afford to do anything expensive.
2. I knew that (partly as a result of 1 above) Jack hadn't intended to go far until next payday.
3. I knew that Jack was meeting me for a drink that evening.
4. I knew that Jack always took an eternity to get ready.
5. I deduced from all of the above (Holmes would surely have been proud of me!) that Jack really couldn't be far away.
6. I knew that the dream showed Jack drowning, so he had to be somewhere with water.

An imaginary lightbulb in my brain suddenly appeared and glowed brightly! Jack was in Crosby and the place with the most water in Crosby was the swimming pool at Crosby Leisure Centre! Of course, it was so obvious now, why hadn't I thought of it before?

Admittedly, it did seem unlikely that Jack could drown at Crosby Leisure Centre. Not only did they have teams of lifeguards watching the pool, but Jack was an excellent swimmer. All those years of swimming lessons had led to us both being able to swim a mile, retrieve bricks from the bottom of the pool and save people's lives in our pyjamas! But Sherlock Holmes' creed accepted that the truth might be improbable, so I had to investigate the swimming pool.

Crosby Leisure Centre wasn't too far away from Blundell Drive, but that day it felt like I was running a marathon as I pounded my way over the Mersey Road railway bridge and down Mariners Road. I burst into reception and through the barriers which led to the corridor to the pool. The receptionist looked up and muttered a token "Hey, what are you doing?" after me, before losing interest and going back to filing her nails.

I ran along the corridor, through the men's changing room and out to the pool. One of the lifeguards shouted at me, "Can't you read, you mustn't wear outdoor shoes in this area," but I ignored him. This was a matter of life and death and there was no time to be putting shoes off and on.

I scanned the poolside area but could not see Jack. I scanned the swimmers but again could not see my brother. I was more than a little scared as I peered through the clear blue water to see if anyone was in trouble beneath the surface, but thankfully there was no one there. I breathed a big sigh of relief.

I felt a hand on my shoulder. It couldn't be, could it? I turned my head slowly, not wanting my hope to be shattered, but when I looked at the man standing next to me, it was most definitely not Jack.

"I've told you already, you can't wear outdoor shoes here," said the lifeguard, "but are you ok, you don't look right?"
"Sorry, sorry," was all I could manage as I turned and slowly trudged dejectedly back through the changing room.

My initial feeling of elation that Jack was not lying dead at the bottom of the swimming pool had quickly evaporated, but was now replaced with confusion. If Jack was not here, then where could he be? I had run out of ideas and even the great Sherlock Holmes had let me down.

I needed help and there was only one man for the job. If I was going to save Jack, I had to find my best friend Jasper!

Chapter Twenty Two

I knew exactly where to find Jasper on a Saturday afternoon.

As a child, Jasper's main hobby had been judo, at which he had demonstrated a natural aptitude. As a teenager, Jasper had risen rapidly through the grades until he had achieved his ultimate ambition of becoming a black belt.

As an adult, however, Jasper was looking for a different challenge. He needed to lose some weight and was also seeking a more sociable sport. Jasper had recently 'discovered' tennis and joined the lovely Glampion Tennis Club in the posh part of Crosby known as Blundellsands. Despite being tucked away behind some grand old mansions, the club boasted seven tennis courts and a fabulous clubhouse.

Jasper had settled in quickly, embracing both the tennis and the social life of the club. He had even been invited to join a team who played in the local league. As you might expect from its location, the team was comprised of lawyers, doctors and other professionals. They even had the smart little man I had watched doing sign language in the corner of the television screen for deaf viewers, the one with the fantastic facial expressions who really gets into the subject matter that he's interpreting.

What did surprise me was that the average age of the team was considerably older than I had expected. The team was known at the club as the G5 and I kept teasing Jasper that the 'G' stood for geriatric!

Anyway, I knew that the G5 squad were taking lessons from the Glampion's friendly Scottish coach. Len Sanders had once taught the famous Wimbledon champion Angus McMurray and the G5 were hoping that some of that magic would rub off on them and propel them up the league.

So I ran again, this time through the subway at the station and along Dowhills Road to the Glampion. Sure enough, there were Len Sanders and the G5 squad, including Jasper.

"Jasper, I need you," I called through the wire fence that surrounded the tennis courts, "it's an emergency!"

Jasper made his excuses to Len and the others and came over to join me in the car park. Such was the team spirit of the G5, however, that they all came over to see what was wrong. A greying but distinguished middle-aged man, who seemed to be their leader, offered to help. I was delighted to know that I had so many people at my disposal, but until I knew what my next move was I didn't know how to make use of them. I explained that I just needed Jasper, but that I would let them know if in due course we needed more manpower.

Jasper and I sat down on one of the benches in front of the clubhouse and I explained my dilemma. Jasper was of the course the only person in the world who knew and believed in my special power. I sometimes wondered whether Jasper ever doubted my gift and whether he was simply humouring me, but right now that didn't matter so long as he could help me save Jack.

When I had finished telling Jasper about my predicament, he thought for a moment, narrowed his eyes and then opened his mouth very purposefully. I was ready to hear something thoughtful and helpful. I was wrong.

"Jasper say, to see one has only to look."
"Jasper, how exactly does that help me?" I was almost shouting at my best friend. "I've been looking everywhere, but I still can't see Jack anywhere."
"Sorry Jimmy, it's the best I can do. But, hang on a minute, what did you say about Jack being underwater?"
"Yes, it's about the only thing I know for sure, but I tried the swimming pool and he wasn't there, so where else could he be?"
"Think about it Jimmy, we're only a long stone's throw from the prom, the beach and ….."

"The sea!" I interrupted. "How could I have been so stupid, of course, he's in trouble on the beach. Quick, we've got to get down to the prom, now."

It was certainly plausible that Jack might be on the beach. I knew he had to be close to home and the beach had always been a special place for both of us. And it was free!

And if he was on the beach, then it was plausible that he could have got into trouble. It never ceased to surprise me how many people did get into trouble on the beach. Barely a week went by without Nefty Sweeney writing yet another news story in the Crosby Bugle about one or more people going out for a walk on the beach and needing to be rescued.

You see, if you walk too far out from the prom the sand becomes soft and you start to sink down into it, until eventually you sink so far that you can't move yourself and you need to be rescued. There are also lots of channels and currents, so that when the tide comes in it is possible to be walking on dry sand but to find that the tide has cut off your route back to shore. I had found myself trapped on these 'islands' many times when playing on the beach as a child, but had always managed to make it back to safety before the water had got more than ankle deep.

The number of incidents had increased in recent years since the iron men had arrived. There were more visitors now, and many were tempted further out onto the beach than was safe by their desire to say hello to the furthest iron men.

It had therefore surprised many local residents when Crosby's coastguard station had been closed down by the austerity government as part of a cost reduction programme. Nefty Sweeney had been particularly outspoken in his (or her) opposition to the closure in a series of articles in the Crosby Bugle. The building was now home to a surf school, a small branch of Starbucks and a gift shop which sold small plastic replicas of the iron men, soft cuddly iron men and postcards of, you've guessed it, the iron men.

To save people from themselves, we had recently acquired a new red and yellow hut down by the old coastguard station. The flag flying above the hut and the signboard outside announced that the hut was operated by the RNLI and the hut was staffed by two teenage boys, Mickey and Donald.

Now I had always associated the RNLI with lifeboats (after all, that is what the L in RNLI stands for), but Mickey and Donald were not the custodians of some inflatable lifeboat. Instead, they each had a red surfboard and on the beach below the hut stood a quad bike on which they enjoyed speeding up and down the beach. Once in a while they even used it to rescue some poor pensioner who had got themselves trapped in the sinking sand.

In my excitement at finally knowing where Jack was, I jumped to my feet and began to run out of the car park and straight down to the sea.

Chapter Twenty Three

I had barely left the car park when Jasper called me back.

"Hold on Jimmy. Jasper say, a man without a plan is like an express train without wheels … he gets nowhere fast!

"There's about two miles of coastline between Seaforth Docks and the River Alt estuary at Hightown. Even if we're right that Jack's trapped on the beach, we can't cover the whole beach between two of us. But I've got an idea!"

Jasper's idea involved mobilising the G5 to help us search the beach. Within two minutes, several cars had sped off to scour different areas of the beach. Player of the Year Reg O'Norris had driven his big silver BMW to the Marine Park in Waterloo, the team captain drove his people carrier to the beach behind the Leisure Centre and the small man from the television gave Jasper and me a lift to the car park by the coastguard station.

I had never seen anyone sit on a booster seat when driving before. Until Jasper had discovered the Glampion and met Teddy Dingle, I had always assumed that the BBC hired normal sized sign language experts and just made them look small in the corner of the screen. Now it struck me that they must deliberately seek out pint-sized people for those jobs.

But, right now, all that mattered was that Teddy was taking us to the beach. We all breathed a sigh of relief as we sped straight over the level crossing at Hall Road railway station without having to wait, and thirty seconds later we pulled into the car park.

All the time we were in the car, I kept seeing Jack. He was still underwater but this time he wasn't upright, he was lying down on the bottom with his eyes closed. I couldn't tell if he was still breathing. The dreams were warning me that if I didn't find Jack soon, it would be too late.

When we got out of the car, I told Jasper to take Teddy north, on the path towards Hightown. Since only Jasper and I knew what Jack looked like, it seemed to make sense for us to split up.

"Jasper, I'm scared," I admitted before we went our separate ways, "I don't think I can do this."
"Jasper say, whether you think you can do something or whether you think you can't, either way you're probably right. So, believe in yourself, Jimmy. Good luck!"

Jasper and Teddy headed north and I ran the other way to the RNLI hut, where Mickey and Donald were enjoying a cup of tea.

"You've got to help me," I spluttered as I burst through the door.

"Of course," said Mickey, "but do join us for a cup of tea first."

"Everything always seems better after a nice cup of tea," added Donald.

Normally I would have agreed with them, but not today.

"No," I said firmly, "there's no time for tea, my brother's stuck somewhere on this beach and we need to find him before he drowns."

"Why didn't you say?!" exclaimed Donald, finally finding his sense of urgency, "come on Mickey, somebody needs us!"

"Right you are Donald," confirmed Mickey, "to the Batmobile!"

"The Batmobile?" I queried.

"It's what he calls the quad bike," explained Donald.

The two of them dived out of the hut, jumped onto the quad bike and sped off across the sand.

"Wait for me!" I shouted after them, but it was no use, they couldn't hear me over the noise of the engine.

So, Mickey and Donald had gone one way and Jasper and Teddy had gone the other way. I was on my own, again. I was annoyed with Mickey and Donald, but I didn't have time to dwell on that now. I had to find Jack. But where could he be on this long beach?

Chapter Twenty Four

I strode towards the water's edge. At low tide the water could be several hundred metres away from the promenade, but now it was barely fifty metres away and advancing rapidly towards the sea wall. In another twenty minutes, the water would be lapping over the top of the wall and splashing the dogwalkers and the mums with prams.

And drowning my poor brother!

I stared in every direction, scanning the horizon for signs of life. Wait, was that him over there? Or over there? I kept seeing bodies in the sea, but every time I looked it was just another iron man. It was always going to be difficult enough trying to find Jack in this vast expanse of sea and sand, without being distracted by a hundred iron men.

I waded out into the water. My shoes, socks and trousers were wet and cold but I didn't care. I kept looking. And looking. And looking. Jasper's words echoed around my head. What was it that he had said, to see one had only to look. To see, one had only to look.

As I looked out to sea, I suddenly became conscious that I was not alone.

In truth, I heard him before I saw him. I'm not sure what you could call the sound he was making, but it fell somewhere between singing, chanting and humming, as if someone was engaging in some ancient and mystic ritual. Having been abruptly disturbed from my thoughts, I swung round towards the source of the strange music. And that's when I saw him.

Interesting rather than handsome, the man possessed a full head of unkempt curly brown hair and a full but similarly wild beard. His facial features were soft and kind and he had the kind of twinkly eyes that are usually the exclusive preserve of favourite uncles. He wore a bold Paisley-patterned shirt and some old dungarees. In one hand he held a paintbrush, while the other grasped a bottle held high in the air above his head. And he was dancing, not a wild jig but slow deliberate moves that matched the rhythm of his music.

A short distance away from the man, a red and white candy-striped deckchair of the traditional English variety sat on the damp sand. In front of the deckchair was an easel, on which the man had evidently been painting. But this was no amateur artist attempting to capture the magnificence of a Crosby sunset behind the iron men and the windfarm. No, this was a man on a mission, a fact revealed by the laptop perched precariously on top of the deckchair.

In fact, whilst the usual features of the Sefton coastline had been faithfully replicated on the canvas, the primary feature of the painting did not exist in real life. For the painting was in fact the first design draft of a proposal to construct a row of beach huts along the sea wall at beach level, and there they all were in pastel shades of blue, green, red, yellow and pink.

The man clearly had a unique approach to his work and the dancing appeared to be designed to summon up his own creative spirit.

"Bob?" I asked, but the man took no notice of me and continued with his weird routine. Was I imagining him too? Had I finally lost my mind completely? Or perhaps his trance-like state did not permit interruptions.

As I turned away from Bob, I saw it. At first it didn't strike me as unusual, just another iron man standing waist deep in the Irish Sea. But then I noticed that he was pointing. Iron men don't point, you see, they all hold their hands straight down at their sides. But this one was definitely pointing.

"Jasper say, when a finger is pointing, only a fool looks at the finger!"

That sounded like Jasper, but surely I wasn't imagining voices now as well, was I? I span round and there was Jasper, or at least it looked like Jasper, but right now I couldn't be sure what was real and what was not.

Chapter Twenty Five

"Jasper, is that really you?" I asked, as if an imaginary Jasper was likely to tell me the truth anyway.

"Yes, it's me," responded Jasper, who I had now concluded was real, "I saw Mickey and Donald speed off without you and I was worried about leaving you on your own. But what is that iron man pointing at?"

We both looked at the pointing iron man and then we both looked at where he was pointing. About fifty yards further out to sea the waves were breaking against something that wasn't an iron man. Something that was moving, just.

"Quick," I called to Jasper, "follow me!"

By a combination of walking and swimming we struggled against the current until we reached the object in the sea. Almost entirely submerged, I could see now that it was the top of a head. But not just any old head, it was Jack's head. Every now and then a hand would emerge from the water and wave frantically. Jack was still alive!

"Hold on Jack, we're nearly there!" I called, as if a submerged Jack would be able to hear me.

I was first to reach Jack. I thought that if I could lift him up to the surface then he would be able to breathe. I put my arms around him and tried to lift him, but it was no good. I tried again, but Jack just wouldn't budge. I was not going to be beaten, I had lived for years with the guilt that perhaps I could have saved Uncle Mo and I was not prepared to fail my brother at the hour of his greatest need.

"Give me a hand," I called to Jasper, "we need to get his head above the water but he's stuck fast in the sand. If we both grab him and pull together, we might be able to shift him. But keep moving, if you stay still you'll sink in the sand too. Right, are you ready, one...two...three...pull!"

Jasper and I pulled with all our might. Slowly but surely, we managed to dislodge Jack from his sandy prison and lift him to the surface. Jack coughed and spluttered and water poured from his mouth. Then he took a breath of air such as I had never seen before and have never seen since. Jack was clearly struggling and couldn't speak. I didn't even know if he recognised us or if he even knew what was happening.

We guided Jack back to the safety of the shore. We couldn't lay him out on the sand, which was nearly covered with water, so we carried him up the steps and laid him out on the prom. I rolled Jack onto his side and into the recovery position. More water escaped from Jack's mouth and formed a small pool next to his body.

I realised that a small crowd had gathered around us to see what all the fuss was about. Jack was no longer coughing and spluttering, but I suddenly realised that he was no longer breathing either. I rolled Jack onto his back and pounded his chest hard and fast. I was glad that I had paid attention to those adverts on the television with Vinnie Jones, although looking back I'm worried that I might have sung the words to 'Staying Alive' out loud rather than just in my head.

After what felt like an eternity, Jack started breathing again. Thank God! He still looked awful and wasn't speaking, but at least he was alive! I had never felt so relieved or so happy in my life.

I pulled my mobile phone from my pocket to call for an ambulance, but the salt water had permeated everything I was wearing and had wrecked my phone. I realised for the first time how wet and cold I was, but that wasn't important right now. I asked a sensible looking man in the assembled throng to call for help, which he was more than happy to do. He also took off his coat and placed it over Jack's body to keep him warm until the ambulance arrived.

I glanced over to my best friend who, like me, was shaking and shivering.

"Thanks Jasper," I said, "we did it! We did it! I wasn't sure that we could, but you said we would and we did!"

"Jasper say, success is like baked beans, it comes in cans."

"What?"

"It comes in cans, not in cannots!"

"JASPER!!"

Chapter Twenty Six

I suppose you're wondering whether that's the end of the story? Well, not quite! Full marks to the more observant among you, who had already noticed from your Kindles that you have only completed just over eighty per cent of the book.

Soon after we arrived at the hospital in the ambulance, we were joined by Mum and Dad, who wanted to make sure that Jack and I were all right. They had rung Jemima, who turned up shortly after them and was visibly distressed until we reassured her that Jack was going to be fine.

Jasper and I felt much better once we'd warmed up and changed into dry clothes. The doctors insisted on treating us both for hypothermia and shock, but we were allowed home later that evening.

Jack spent a few days in hospital recovering from his adventure. Fortunately there was no long term damage, although the doctors did say that if Jasper and I had arrived any later then Jack would undoubtedly have died.

I went back to Blundell Drive with Mum and Dad, leaving Jemima to sit with Jack. We gave Jasper a lift and dropped him off on the way. Nobody said much in the car, I think we were all just relieved that things hadn't turned out much worse.

I was also unsure how Mum and Dad would react to the afternoon's events. The last time I had seen them they had refused to take my premonitions seriously. Now that I had proved that I wasn't making things up, would they accept my story, just like that? I was worried that, even after all that had happened today, they would try to find a 'rational' explanation or put it down to 'coincidence'.

It was therefore with some degree of trepidation that I took my place at the dining room table while my Dad made us all a nice pot of tea. When we were all sitting down, nursing a steaming mug of hot tea and tucking into a plate of chocolate digestives, my Mum was first to speak.

"I'm sorry, Jimmy," she began, "but your story just seemed too fantastic to believe. Did you really see Jack drowning?"

And so I told them everything. I told them about the dreams I had seen recently showing Jack's impending disaster. I told them about Dad's broken wrist. I told them about Corky Dog and Rabbit. I even told them about Uncle Mo. And all the time I was speaking, Mum and Dad just listened. I could see from their expressions that this time they believed me, although they were obviously still struggling with the concept that anyone could see the future.

When I had finished, Mum and Dad just looked at me. Why wouldn't they say anything? I guess they had a lot to take in. It reminded me of that day many years ago when I had told Jasper.

When eventually they were ready, it was Dad who spoke, although he was obviously struggling to express himself.

"I'm sorry too, Jimbob," he said, in a voice that was softer and quieter than usual, "I still find it difficult to believe that anyone can see the future, but it's obvious that you're telling the truth. I'm so proud of you and grateful to you for saving Jack's life today. If it wasn't for you, we could be sitting here tonight mourning our son, your brother. And you put your own life at risk to save him. Thank you, Jimbob."

"No worries," I replied, "I'm sure that Jack would have done exactly the same for me if it had been the other way round."

"That's so good to hear," said Dad, "I always hoped that, despite all your differences, when push came to shove you brothers would always be there for each other. Sometimes I've not been so sure that you boys cared enough about each other, but today proves that you do."

I could see tears rolling down my father's cheeks. I had never seen him cry before, but it had been an emotional day for all of us.

"What will you do?" asked Mum.

"Do?"

"Will you tell people what really happened today?"

"I don't know, I haven't thought that far ahead yet. I'm not sure the world is ready for my story yet, and I don't want to be labelled as a freak just when things are really starting to take off for me."

"Try not to worry about that, Jimbob," interrupted Dad, "I'm sure everything will turn out for the best."

I said my goodbyes and wandered back to my own home. It was late and I was ready for my bed, but I couldn't help myself from making a slight detour to the prom. The stars were shining brightly in the clear night sky and a nearly-but-not-quite full moon illuminated the scene. I stood there for maybe five minutes, transfixed by the beach, the sea and the iron men.

My mind was racing as I replayed the day's events over and over again. As I remembered all the bizarre things that had happened, my mind settled on one particularly mysterious detail which had unlocked the puzzle. Mysterious, but impossible. Quite, quite impossible.

But that conundrum would have to wait until tomorrow.

Chapter Twenty Seven

I awoke early the next morning, disturbed by my dreams. I dreamt that Jack was drowning on Crosby beach and I didn't know how to save him.

Then I went to check my mobile phone for any messages. It wasn't working. I wondered whether the SIM card would work in my old phone, so I rummaged around for my old phone and swapped it over. My old phone had no charge, so I rummaged around again until I found its charger, and then I plugged one end into the phone and the other end into the electricity socket.

The phone bleeped once to confirm it was charging and then shortly afterwards it bleeped again to indicate that I had received a text message. I picked up the phone and saw that the message was from Dad:

Hope u got home safely. The hospital called to say Jack had a good night and is feeling better. C u later.

Dad's texts always amused me, with his feeble attempts at text-speak and his insistence on correct grammar. I had given Mum and Dad a mobile phone each after Dad's fall on the ice and, unlike Mum, Dad had embraced the new technology. He was even talking about buying a computer next!

But, hold on a minute, if my new phone wasn't working and Dad was texting me about Jack in hospital then it hadn't all been a dream, it had really happened! You can't blame me for not being sure after all that happened recently.

I stood for a minute or two whilst reality sank in and I remembered the mystery that I needed to solve today. I turned on my iPad and checked that I was right about something.

Then I realised that I was starving. Apart from demolishing half a packet of Mum's chocolate digestives, I hadn't eaten much yesterday in all the excitement. I poured myself an extra large helping of corn flakes and made a mug of really strong black coffee, after which I felt a bit more human.

I showered, got dressed and walked back to the beach. I strode purposefully to where yesterday's adventures had taken place. Fortunately, the tide was a long way out, affording me complete freedom to wander out among the iron men. I used the RNLI hut to align myself and then strode forward towards the horizon.

It was impossible to establish exactly where I had found Jack the previous day. The beach looked so different with the tide out and there was no possibility of footprints since the tide had been in and out again since yesterday's drama. But it had to be somewhere close to where I was walking.

Being careful where I was putting my feet for fear of becoming stuck myself, I explored the area and examined every iron man in the vicinity. Those I could not reach safely I could still observe from my position. They all looked like they should, staring out to sea with their hands at their sides. Yesterday, one of them had definitely been pointing and had helped me to save Jack, but today there was no evidence of this.

Perplexed, I turned round and walked back to the prom, still looking left and right in the hope of seeing the iron man who had guided me to Jack. I popped my head into the RNLI hut, where Mickey and Donald were enjoying a cup of tea.

 "Hello," said Mickey, "have you come back for that cup of tea?"
"Everything always seems better after a cup of tea," added Donald.
"No … erm, not exactly …. oh, go on then," I stuttered.

Mickey poured me a mug of tea and Donald added some milk.

"Is that tea ok for you, it's not a fortnight?" enquired Donald.
"A fortnight?" I queried, feeling suitably confused.
"You know," continued Mickey, "a fortnight … too weak!"

The tea was perfectly fine, but I don't think that pair of jokers really cared what my answer was. In fact, I doubt they heard me as they both guffawed at their own joke. Eventually they calmed down enough to resume something resembling a normal conversation.

"Excellent piece of work yesterday," continued Donald.
"Yes," interrupted Mickey, "have you ever thought of becoming a lifeguard?"
"Thanks," I replied, "and no, I have a job thanks, I'm an architect. Anyway, I was wondering how much you two know about the iron men?"
"Lots!" asserted Mickey.
"Yes," confirmed Donald, "what we don't know about the iron men isn't worth knowing. Did you know, for instance, that each figure is one hundred and eighty-nine centimetres tall?"
"That's six feet two inches in old money," chirped Mickey.
"No, I didn't know that," I admitted, "but what I was wondering is whether it's possible to move them?"
"Move them?" repeated Mickey.
"Well, they did have to move sixteen of them when they made them permanent," advised Donald.
"No, that's not what I meant," I interrupted, "I meant can you change how any individual iron man looks, like maybe raising its arm up or turning its head?"

Mickey and Donald looked at each other and then gave me that look, you know the withering look that's usually reserved for weary mothers to give their children when they keep asking silly questions.

"These aren't action men!" retorted Donald. "They're not poseable figures that you can bend into whatever position you like. Yes, people sometimes dress them up, but you can't reposition the figures themselves. They're six hundred and fifty kilos of solid metal each, you know!"
"That's one thousand four hundred pounds in old money," chirped Mickey.

It really worried me that this pair of jokers had such an important role to play keeping people safe on my beloved beach, but when it came to the iron men they certainly seemed to know their onions. I finished my tea and left them to continue amusing themselves.

On my way back home, I called on Jasper and asked him about the mystery of the pointing iron man.

"I'm sorry Jimmy," Jasper apologised, "but in all the excitement I can't really remember everything that happened. I'm not saying there wasn't an iron man pointing to Jack, I honestly don't remember."
"But you said that when someone is pointing, only a fool looks at their pointing finger, or something like that. Surely you remember saying that?"

"Sorry Jimmy, I don't, although it sounds like the sort of thing Jasper would say. In fact, I know that expression, it's from that great French film with the subtitles, what was it called?"

"I don't remember, I don't think I've seen it. Thanks again for your help, I really couldn't have saved Jack without you."

"Amelie!"

"What?"

"Amelie. The name of that French film. I knew it would come back to me!"

"Great, I'm pleased for you! I was trying to thank you for saving Jack, if you were listening?! It was a remarkable day, but I hope we don't have too many more days like that, I don't think my heart could take it."

"Jasper say, to me every day is a gift … that's why it's called the present!"

"JASPER!!!!!!!!!"

I guessed I'd never know for sure whether the iron man had really been pointing or whether it was my mind – or the dreams – playing tricks on me. I supposed that in the overall scheme of things it didn't really matter, but I was just curious and didn't like not knowing.

So, one mystery left unsolved, one mystery still to solve.

Chapter Twenty Eight

A couple of days later, Jack was allowed home and I think everyone breathed a huge sigh of relief that he was on the mend.

That same day, I received an email at the office from the Crosby Bugle. Apparently, Nefty Sweeney wanted to interview Jack, Jasper and me about Jack's dramatic rescue. As strange as it may sound, and despite my life-long attachment to the Bugle, up to that moment it hadn't dawned on me that we were newsworthy.

After a couple of phone calls to Jack and Jasper and an email exchange with the Bugle, all was arranged for the following day. Arnie said he was happy for me to take the whole day off if necessary, for which I was grateful to him. I wasn't sure that I wanted our story plastered all over the front page, but at least it would allow me to solve one mystery which had bugged me for years.

Finally, after all those years of wondering, we would finally find out whether Nefty Sweeney was a man or a woman!

Chapter Twenty Nine

We were all sitting in Jack's front room when the doorbell rang at ten o'clock the following morning. I literally jumped up and ran to the door, eager to see what the legendary Nefty Sweeney looked like!

I opened the door and found a woman standing on the doorstep. Nefty Sweeney was a woman! And not just a woman, but the most beautiful woman I had ever seen in my life. She was dressed immaculately, her stylish ensemble finished off with a bottle green waistcoat and a necklace of expensive-looking beads.

"Nefty Sweeney?"
"Oh no!," laughed the beautiful woman, "Nefty's just parking the car. I'm Penelope Cordelia, pleased to meet you. Strictly speaking I'm the fashion editor, but I promised Old Nefty that I'd tag along and take some notes."
"Penelope Cordelia," I enjoyed repeating her name. "Hi, I'm Jimmy McLoughlin, please come in and make yourself at home."

As Penelope Cordelia glided past me and entered the house, another figure appeared at the garden gate and walked up the path towards me. The contrast could not have been greater. Penelope was tall, slim and elegant, whilst Nefty gave the appearance of being short, slightly rotund and a little rough around the edges. This was a man who had seen a bit of life!

But what Nefty lacked in looks, he more than made up for in personality. As he approached me, I was greeted with a huge beaming smile and a hand thrust out to greet me.

"Hello young man, I'm Nefty Sweeney," he announced in an unmistakable Northern Irish accent, "and I'm so grateful to you for agreeing to do this interview. You are all going to be celebrities, everyone loves a hero! You know, I was thinking in the car that this is probably the biggest news we've covered since that talented young man from Crosby beat that Jamaican sprinter chappy in the Olympic Stadium. Has Stinkers already gone in?"
"Stinkers?"
"Oh sorry, I mean Penelope Cordelia! How unprofessional of me to use her nickname. You won't tell her, will you? She'd be so embarrassed if she knew I'd called her Stinkers to a complete stranger. Not that we'll be complete strangers by the time we've finished this interview, of course, but you know what I mean!"

When Nefty had finally finished talking, and I had recovered from him referring to the angelic Penelope Cordelia as 'Stinkers', I ushered him inside. If the interviewer had that much to say for himself, I could see that this was going to be a very long session!

The interview was quite illuminating and I was able to fill in many of the details that had hitherto escaped me. Nefty explained that the lifeguards Donald and Mickey had told him that I had mentioned that I was an architect, which was how Nefty had tracked me down to my work address.

Jack explained how he had gone for a walk on the beach to pass the time until meeting me in the evening, but he had walked out too far from the prom and become trapped in the sand. He had tried shouting and waving but had been unable to attract anyone's attention. Normally he would have been able to phone for help, but he had left his mobile phone at home. He was so broke that he had not been able to afford to top up the credit on it. He had struggled to keep upright as the tide rushed in and had just about given up any hope of being rescued when the water became so deep that he could no longer keep his face above water.

Jasper and I then took over the story, explaining how we went looking for Jack and eventually found him on the beach. I didn't want the whole of Crosby thinking I was insane, so I thought it best not to mention the dreams or the mystery of the pointing iron man. But I had underestimated the experienced journalist.

"What I don't understand," Nefty began, sounding like someone out of an episode of some American detective series from the 1970s, maybe Columbo. "What I don't understand, Jimmy, is why you went looking for Jack? He couldn't call you because he didn't have his phone, so how did you know he was in trouble?"

"Erm …. Um ..." I stuttered. I hadn't anticipated that question and was struggling to know how to answer it. How could I have been so stupid?!

"Well," I continued, "I know it sounds a bit bonkers, but I just knew, kind of instinctively, that Jack needed me."

"Wow!" exclaimed Penelope Cordelia, "I've heard about that sort of thing happening between twins, knowing when the other twin is in danger, feeling each other's pain, that sort of thing. It's not quite telepathy, but a sort of empathy that no scientist can explain. But I've never heard of it between brothers who aren't twins before. I guess you two must be pretty close?"

I hesitated before answering. I was too embarrassed to tell the truth about my relationship with Jack. I looked across at Jack and could see that he was facing the exact same quandary. For a split second our eyes met, and Jack smiled at me.

"Of course we are," Jack lied. I hoped that what he really meant was, "Of course we are *now*," but history did not fill me with any particular confidence that things would change, even if I had just saved his life.

"I guess it's true what they say," continued Penelope Codelia, "the mind really is a mysterious and powerful tool."

"Jasper say, to control the body one must first learn to control the mind!" piped up Jasper, not wanting to be outdone on the wisdom front. I hadn't heard Jasper utter that particular wisdom for many years.

"JASPER!!!" Jack and I shouted in unison.

"Hang on a minute," said Nefty, looking excited, "what did you just say, young fellow?"

"Oh, he's got plenty more of those," I chuckled, "I call them 'the wisdoms of Jasper' and there's one for every occasion!"

"Really!" The old journalist's big eyes lit up with excitement.

"You mean someone actually likes my sayings?" laughed Jasper. "Oh happy day!"

And that is how we all became famous local celebrities. The Crosby Bugle loved the 'psychic siblings' angle and the story ran for several weeks while readers wrote in with their own tales evidencing the special bond that exists between siblings.

My favourite story involved the twin sisters who wrote in that they had once turned up to the same wedding wearing identical dresses. Now that may not in itself sound too remarkable, but what made the story for me was the letter in the following week's edition from their older sister explaining that it had in fact been her wedding … at which her younger twin sisters had been her bridesmaids!

In fact, we became so well-known that a few months later we were invited to switch on the Crosby Christmas lights by local community group 'A Better Crosby'. Alongside my hero Hank Bovril-Joyce, of course!

Epilogue

Everything I've written about happened some time ago now.

I've only had one special dream since then, which happened soon after the beach incident and which felt like a reward for saving Jack, even if it didn't reveal any winning lottery numbers. The fact that I haven't had a premonition for a while doesn't mean I'll never have another one, but recently I've started wondering whether it was all leading up to that one episode.

I've also been reflecting on what I have learnt from those times. I've learnt a lot about family, friendship, belief … and myself.

Lesson One: Jack

Despite our differences and the rivalry of our youth, we have come to realise that we have more in common than either of us would like to admit. I saved Jack without hesitation and I have no doubt that he would have done the same for me. We may never have become as inseparable as Mum and Dad would have liked before the beach incident, but we have now put the past behind us and become firm friends. It's a shame that it took nearly losing Jack to make us appreciate each other, but better late than never, I suppose.

Lesson Two: Jasper

Written off by many people as a fool (including me sometimes, I'm embarrassed to admit), Jasper demonstrated the value of true friendship. The only person who was prepared to believe my secret without proof, Jasper followed me into a dangerous situation without question or hesitation … because he was my friend. Jack especially recognises Jasper's role in his rescue and has come to regard Jasper as a loyal and trusted friend.

Lesson Three: Mum and Dad

After periodically resenting my parents for their lack of faith in me, I have realised that their failure to believe my secret was a perfectly reasonable reaction. I accept now that they only ever wanted the best for me, and for me and Jack to be friends. It feels great that they now know and accept the truth and the bonds between us that we established when I was a child are stronger than ever.

Lesson Four: Me

The obvious thing to say is that I have realised that I am far stronger, physically and mentally, than I had ever imagined.

Perhaps less obvious, and harder for me to accept, was my realisation of how much my family mean to me. We may not have always been particularly close before the incident at the beach, but it seems that we were all just waiting for an opportunity to come together.

On the work front, the New Liver Building is emerging from the rubble of the old Royal Liver Building. An innovative and groundbreaking design, it is not only visually stunning but will also generate more than one hundred per cent of its own requirements for energy, heat, hot water and air conditioning, leaving no carbon footprint whatsoever and in fact generating surplus energy which will be fed into the national grid. Although it is not yet finished, the new building is already widely tipped to win several prestigious awards, not just for design but also for sustainability.

I have been asked in several interviews how I came up with such a radical but beautiful design. My simple answer I tell them every time is that it came to me in a dream. The interviewers assume I am being coy or modest, if only they knew that I was telling the truth!

Dad has recently retired from his job in Liverpool city centre. I don't suppose I'll ever find out now exactly what he did! Since Mum and Dad now have so much more time on their hands, they have both started helping out at the Crosby Area Foodbank, providing emergency food parcels for those in need. It's a fantastic cause and I am very proud of them for getting involved.

Jasper has profited from our encounter with the Crosby Bugle. 'The Wisdoms of Jasper' is now a popular weekly feature in the newspaper and this year Jasper became the first person in history to dislodge Hank Bovril-Joyce as 'Crosby's coolest person'.

Jasper wasn't the only person to benefit from that meeting. I am delighted to announce that Penelope Cordelia and I have recently become engaged. She really is the love of my life and we are getting married next summer. Maybe one day I will finally discover how she acquired the nickname 'Stinkers'! In fact, it will be a double wedding, since Jack and Jemima have also decided to tie the knot.

It goes without saying that the wedding will take place at St Cuthbert's. Father Shivijan, the only possible man for the job, will be doing the honours. No longer the energetic young priest that I remember from my childhood, he has served our community for a generation. In light of recent reconciliations, Jack has asked me to be his best man and I am delighted to have been able to ask him to be mine. I think Jasper was secretly hoping for that particular job, but he understands the situation and accepts it, as true friends do. I'm conscious that I will need to look my very best on the big day, since I can only imagine how elegant and stylish Penelope Cordelia will look in a wedding dress. I just hope that Nefty Sweeney, who Penelope has asked to give her away, tidies himself up for the occasion!

Bob the invisible man unfortunately cannot attend our wedding. Apparently it coincides with an important mystical ceremony at

Stonehenge that he really cannot miss. He has however presented us with a most unique wedding present, the large and well-wrapped rectangular present turning out to be the painting he had been busy with on the beach that fateful day.

The wooden beach huts are of course now a reality, brought to life by local resident John Sunny, a Geordie who now lived in Crosby. John was a most interesting character, since he worked primarily as a carpenter but was probably more famous in the locality for raising bees. Many a time the trains on the Liverpool to Southport line were delayed or cancelled because John's bees were swarming, and questions had been asked in the House of Commons the year that trains had to be suspended completely for the whole of the May bank holiday.

I was delighted to receive Bob's painting. Not only was it a most beautiful creation, but I had come to love the brightly painted beach huts as much as the iron men. The painting also contained the key to the one remaining mystery. I didn't notice it at first, but one day when I was studying the painting in detail, I noticed something quite remarkable. At first I thought I must be imagining it, but when I looked again it was still there. Although the painting had been produced first and foremost to portray how the beach huts might look, Bob had captured every detail of that day on the beach. And that included every detail of the iron men.

When I looked at the painting, I could clearly see that one iron man was not standing with his arms down at his side like all the others, but was pointing out to sea. It was incredible to see and proved that I had not been imagining things. One of the iron men really had directed me to save Jack and Bob's painting proved it. Not that anyone would believe me of course, but I knew and that was all that mattered.

After the wedding, we are honeymooning in Egypt and Saudi Arabia. It's an adventure I feel compelled to undertake and I guess it's a sort of Uncle Mo pilgrimage, taking in many of the exotic and historic places he enthralled me with when I was a boy. My only disappointment is that we won't be able to visit Mecca, since only Muslims are allowed to enter that particular city.

For me, little Jimmy McLoughlin with the red hair and freckles, the future now looks brighter than it ever has before. What could possibly go wrong?

Appendix: The top 20 'Wisdoms of Jasper'

Jasper say:

It is only in darkness that we can see the stars

Life without football is like a blunt pencil … pointless

To see, one has only to look

A man without a plan is like an express train without wheels … he gets nowhere fast

It is a wise man who learns from his own mistakes, but a wiser man who learns from the mistakes of others

No man can know the future

The mind is like a parachute, it works best when it is open

Success is like baked beans … it comes in cans (not in cannots)

The man who gains a reputation for getting up at dawn can lie in bed until midday

To me, every day is a gift… that's why it's called the present

To control the body, one must first learn to control the mind

The early bird may get the worm, but it's the second mouse who gets the cheese

No peas for the wicked

Whether you think you can do something or whether you think you can't, either way you're probably right

Anywhere is within walking distance, if you have the time

Why do today what can be put off until tomorrow?

Only a fool can get lost on a straight road

It's a small world, but you wouldn't want to Hoover it

If a boy wants his dreams to come true, at some point he must wake up

When a finger is pointing, only a fool looks at the finger

6298116R00085

Printed in Great Britain
by Amazon.co.uk, Ltd.,
Marston Gate.